BOOM BOOM'S LAST CALL

BOOM BOOM'S LAST CALL

A Novel

Jeff Houlahan

For Kim. Always.

Chapter One

Her name should have been Gehenna…or Golgotha—she left me scored and scoured, spent and spiked and shit-talking God. She was a skullfucker, full-time and full-on. Now, she was dead. And I was their guy. Bitter ex-boyfriend. There were moments I was half-convinced I killed her. Except I didn't.

Dasha.

Her name.

I needed a glass of water and a Percocet. Or two. Or three. But fucked if I was going to let them know that. The door to the interview room pushed open.

Good cop—dark hair with a little bit of silver, early forties but lean and fit, movie star-handsome, aging like oiled wood. On my best day, I should look so good.

"Hey, Flint. Can we get you something? Water? Coffee?"

"I'm good."

"You don't look so good."

Beveled edge to the words. Maybe he and his partner had switched hats.

"Wish I could say the same—can I get a Coke?"

"What?"

"Coke. Soft drink."

"Sure. No problem. Anything else? Pizza all-dressed? Back rub?"

Yep. New hat. He scraped the chair along the hard, pebbled floor, pulling it back to sit down. Slip-resistant in case they had to get into it.

"So, tell me again when you last saw your girlfriend?"

"Ex."

"Right. Ex-girlfriend."

"Three weeks ago. Give or take."

"That when she dumped you?"

"In a manner of speaking."

"I'm not following."

We had been through this once already, but I knew the drill.

"She showed up at the club where I work—with some older guy. Sharp-dressed guy—Brioni and Testoni's."

"Older?"

"Bout your age—maybe a few years younger."

He grinned. Not mean, digging the dig. He wasn't cut out for bad cop.

"That's when she told you to move along?"

I smiled…but it was tougher than I expected.

"She didn't need to say anything—he used her ass for a hand warmer most of the night."

"So, you kicked his?"

"He got drunk, made a scene at the bar, and I tossed him."

"Broke his nose."

"You've got the report. He swung at me twice before I laid a hand."

He looked me over.

"You're not the kind we usually see on the door."

Five nine and one hundred sixty pounds—I knew what he meant. We stared across the table at each other, and then he raised his eyebrows… So?

"That was a question?"

He couldn't help smiling again. He pointed to a spot over my left eyebrow.

"How did you get that? Tossin' the wrong guy?"

"Nah. Rough ride."

"Come again?"

"Rode rough stock for a living. Got hung up."

I ran my thumb over the scar—couldn't help it.

"Hoof or hardpack—we never did figure it out."

"What the fuck are you talking about?"

"Rough stuff. Broncs. Bulls. You know…rodeo."

"You're kidding me? Thought you were from Brooklyn?"

"Long story."

He leaned back in his chair staring at me, balancing so the back two legs were touching the floor.

"Well, I'll be damned. A real-life concrete, bright lights, downtown cowboy. You any good?"

I shrugged.

"It was a living."

I had been top-ten for three years and won the whole thing the year before I got run over—made more than a million dollars and couldn't hang on to any of it. It still hurt—in more ways than one. He let the chair tip forward onto the floor and got back on track.

"Was that the last time you had any contact with Dasha?"

Dasha. Hearing her name was like a fist in the belly—I felt something give.

The cop knew it wasn't the last time. They had the police report.

"Last time I saw her?"

"Not what I asked."

I waved at the manila folder.

"You've got it there."

"I want to hear it from you."

I looked down at my hands and back up. He was watching me. Not smiling…not even a bit. Narrow, focused, hungry, trying to get past skin and skull, spoon into the soft stuff.

Fuck you.

"I went by her apartment. I wa…"

"When was this?"

I looked at the folder before answering.

"Four nights ago. Thursday night."

He nodded for me to continue.

"I wanted to talk to her."

"To say what?"

"I don't know. The usual shit you say when you're breaking up. Why? You bitch. Same old, same old."

What do they call it? The long goodbye. From almost the first minute, I could feel the end. It had been like being a kid sitting at the side of the road, watching the cars drive through on their way to somewhere else. Spotting them from far away, a spark and glint through the heat haze, the thrill rising from beneath your belly, waving as hard as you could and laughing as the car drew closer, long and shiny and black, and then it was by and gone, and you tossed a hand at the trail of dust as the nickel dropped cold and hard.

She was the kind of girl who was looking for the backdoor before she knew your last name.

I looked up. He must have said something.

"Wake up, Flint, are you with me? I said what happened next?"

I shook my head clear.

"You know what happened—she wouldn't talk to me, and I wouldn't leave, and eventually she called the cops. I got hauled downtown."

"Did you threaten her?"

"I don't remember. I was drunk."

"You do that often?"

"What? Get drunk and yell at my ex-girlfriend?"

"Just the first part."

"Somewhere between too often and not often enough."

"She claimed you threatened to kill her."

"I don't remember. Doesn't sound like my style."

"Did you go back there Sunday night?"

I shook my head and shifted in the chair, stretching my left leg, levering out some of the ache.

"No. I was working—ten to three."

"On a Sunday night?"

"It's a big night for the bar crowd—waiters, line cooks, bartenders. Their party night."

"Where do you work?"

"You know this, detective. Boom Boom's. Off Roosevelt."

"Busy night?"

"Crazy. They bring in the banda bands. Mostly Mexican clientele. Weekend cowboys."

"Any trouble?"

"No more than usual. We had to run a couple of knuckleheads. Nothing that broke skin."

We both looked around as the door clicked open. His partner stuck his head in, gave a quick nod, and ducked back out.

"Gimme a second, Flint, I'll be right back."

I looked around. The interview room was the usual—grim, rough pebbled floor, yellowed and scuffed, cameras in the corners, one-way window along one wall, cheap plastic table bolted to the floor, and cheap plastic chairs that weren't.

I tried not to think of the pictures I had seen—they had slid a crime scene photo across the table at me early in the interview looking for a reaction—she had taken one to the back of the head, neat going in, splintered meat coming out. And that had been the ending, somebody had worked on her for a while before they had killed her. Somebody who had been pissed.

I tried not to think of her, rag and bone on a stained rug. She had been crazy—a human Catherine wheel, spinning and sparking, either on fire or burnt. Trying not to think of her was like talking to the wind, like keeping still on the cracking ice, like trying to smile against the lash, against the gas. It was a clown's prayer. It was a waste of time.

The door opened, and both cops came back in. The older, pouchy black cop held the door open. The other one spoke.

"Your manager confirmed your story. You can go, Flint. But we may need to talk to you again."

I stood up, and my bad leg gave, and I had to grab at the table.

"You okay?"

I nodded.

"Foot fell asleep."

The black cop spoke as I went by.

"I still think you're good for this. Just because you weren't there doesn't mean you're not our guy."

He spoke again when I was almost at the end of the hall.

"We're not done with you, Einstein."

He wasn't being ironic. That was me. Einstein Flint. Another long story.

Chapter Two

"Hey, L'il Mike."

"What's doin', bra? Sorry to hear about Dasha."

Miquel Carillo—L'il Mikey—bar back at Boom's. His real job was to bounce but Freddie liked to keep the big guys off the door—figured that putting weight on the door was like tossing seal meat in a shark tank. And L'il Mikey was big. Biggest Mexican I had ever seen.

I slid up onto a stool. Mikey leaned down, pulled out a cold beer and held it up. I shook my head.

"I'm on tonight."

He crouched to slide bottles into the bottom fridges.

"Heard you got pulled in."

I could see the top of his head.

"Yeah."

"Fucked up, man."

"I'll say."

The room was cool, but my neck and face felt hot, and my eyeballs ground left and right like the sockets had been seeded with sand and salt. But I couldn't keep them still. Sleep had been hard to come by.

"You remember the guy she was with that last night she was in?"

Li'l Mikey stood to pull another case off the bar onto the floor beside him but didn't look over.

"Yeah, tough to forget. Bangin'. Too old for her, but he was pulling it off."

Now, he looked at me and smiled.

"But no instincts and a heavy bleeder—bad combo. You messed up his gear, man. You think he's in this?"

I shrugged.

"Who knows. Got to start somewhere. Freddie in?"

"Up in the office."

I slid off the stool and started towards the back.

"Hey, Ones?"

I turned back. He didn't say anything.

"What you got, Mikey?"

He shrugged.

"You know, eh? Dasha? She was into some crazy shit."

The front room was long and narrow, with a dark wooden bar running almost the length of one wall and plain round wood tables scattered down the other side. It opened into a larger room in back with a stage and a dance floor, and the same kind of tables scattered around the outer edge of the room. There was a door behind the stage with a set of steep, narrow stairs leading up to the top-floor office. My knee clicked on every step. The office was little more than an attic hutch—even I had to duck to get under the door frame.

Freddie waved me in.

"Ones. Come in. Come on in—what a fucking mess. Dasha. Such a sweet girl. I can't believe it. This city…it's a fucking sewer."

Freddie Riley was a one-off—purebred Irish, red hair and freckles paired with big western belt buckles, a neck scarf, and a beret—he looked like Alfred E. Newman auditioning for the lead in Che—The Musical. But he had given me a job when I needed one.

"You got a minute, Freddie?"

"For you, Einstein? As long as you need. A fucking tragedy, this. And hauling you in—it's a fucking disgrace. I told them when they called—are you fucking crazy…he was here all night. This guy, kill a woman? Are you kidding me? He's old school—kick your ass, pal. But a woman? Not a fucking chance."

"Thanks for that, Freddie. It got me out of a jam."

He waved his hand.

"Least I could do. You're my guy. I know I can count on you to keep things cool, copacetic, con…"

"Freddie, did you know the guy that Dasha was—the guy I got into it with?"

That stopped him.

'That wasn't one of your best nights, Ones. That could have cost me money. We're lucky he didn't come after us."

"Freddie, it's a simple question—did you know the guy?"

He shook his head, pissed that I was stepping in, not letting him slide, but not sure what to do about it.

"First timer. Never saw him before. Didn't look like our usual crowd."

"He paid with a card—you'll have his slip here somewhere."

I waved at the pile of papers on his desk. Freddie pushed his chair away from the desk until it bumped against the back wall and tried to swing his legs up onto the desk, but there wasn't quite enough room, and he gave up.

"What makes you think this is the guy? Why this guy?"

I shrugged.

"I'm not saying it's this guy, Freddie, but I've got nothing else to go on right now."

"Why do you need anything? Let the cops do their job. She wasn't even your girl anymore. You're shoveling wind, son."

"Go through the slips, Freddie. I'm not going to make trouble for the guy if he's not in this—I want a name…check him out."

He rolled his chair back into the desk, and the wheels sounded thin and hollow on the worn wooden floor. He puffed out his cheeks and exhaled in a thin stream.

"You know I fired her, don't you? She didn't quit."

I nodded.

"You know why, too, don't you?"

He didn't wait for an answer.

"She was moving product, Ones. And not just weed. Coke and Molly…Oxy when she could get it. Not a lot, but regular. I couldn't have that in the bar. It wasn't her, it's the guys that come with it. The guys that are fronting her the stuff. Once they worm their way in, they're like fucking roaches—you can't get them out without torching the fucking place."

I knew this, too. It wasn't like the owner ever knew anything before the floor. We all knew that Dasha had been dealing, but there was hardly a bar in town that didn't do a little trade. And there hadn't been anybody behind her. At least not while I was with her. She didn't sell a lot—what she could buy from a few small-time dealers she knew and flip to make a few hundred extra a week.

"That's helpful, Freddie, but I'm looking for a name on the guy."

"I let her pretend she quit—so it wouldn't screw her up for getting another job. You get a rep for dealing; you're done in this business."

I kept my face still. Getting fired from Boom's was never going to stop her from getting hired—she was funny, snap-a-whip smart, and stunning—she wouldn't even need to fill out an application.

"I understand, Freddie. Can I get the guy's name?"

"Jesus H, you're a dog on a bone, Flint."

He looked at me across the desk, and I stared back. He flinched first.

"Ah, shit. What can it hurt? She was a good girl. It's a fucking shame what happened."

He gestured at the pile on his desk.

"It's in here somewhere. I haven't had a chance to file for a couple of months. What day was it?"

I didn't need to do any calculations—I had done them, and the date was stuck in my head.

"Three weeks back. May seventeenth."

" I remember…cops showed up after one, so he would have paid around when? Twelve-thirty?"

I nodded.

"Let's say between twelve-fifteen and twelve-forty-five."

He thumbed through the papers, narrowing them down to three or four sheets, flipping back and forth a few times before settling on the page. I wanted to reach across the desk and rip them out of his hands but didn't. How do you run a successful business without understanding numerical order?

"Here we go—I've got four names between those times, but only two are guys, and another is a company card."

I grabbed a pen lying on his desk, looking around for something to write on. Freddie ripped a post-it note free and passed it across.

"Don't bring any of this back on me. Don't go fucking this guy up unless you really have something on him."

"Don't worry, Freddie. You won't get any on you."

He nodded.

"OK. Antonio Solis, Thomas Perry, and a place called Benoit Asset Management."

I wrote them down, put the pen back on the desk, and stood up.

"Thanks, Freddie. I should get back downstairs."

He nodded.

"Have a good shift, Ones. Give this some time. It'll get better."

* * *

I caught Bobby V's eye and nodded at the guy on the edge of the dance floor. We were standing about fifty feet apart, Bobby at the end of the bar talking to a regular and me near the door, watching as people came in. Bobby craned to look over the crowd of people, saw the guy and nodded back. I was glad Bobby was on. He was steady and calm but ready—shaking the ache out of his fist before the other guy knew the fight had started.

Bobby came at him from the dance floor side, and I worked my way through the crowd along the wall. The guy was big. Not show-room big—cut, buffed, and brittle—this guy was marbled beef through the chest and shoulders—gut, butt, and thigh thick—he had lifted heavy stuff all week long and didn't care if his slacks and shirt hung right. He had the woman by her upper arm and was smiling mean, the kind of smile that always came behind stink sweat, acetylened adrenalin, and an offensive bulge against her belly.

Bobby took a spot to the side, feet shoulder-width apart and hands crossed. The guy caught the movement as people moved out of the way, and he glanced at Bobby, looked away, then back as recognition worked its way through the liquor haze and crossed wires. But I spoke first.

"Sir, can we buy you a drink?"

That wasn't what he had expected.

"A drink?"

"Yessir, we would like to buy you a drink. We do this every night—pick a couple of customers at random and buy them the drink of their choice. Follow us over to the bar, and we'll set you up."

Sometimes it worked.

"Fuck off, boyos. I'm busy right now, and I can buy my own drinks."

This wasn't going to be one of those times. He turned back to the woman, his fist still around her upper arm, her pretty face pale and wan even under the dance floor lighting.

"Sir, I'm going to have to ask you to let go of the lady."

He didn't even look back at us.

"I told you boys to f…"

I hit him first. Hard and in the throat. You have to get it right because you can crush a man's windpipe, maybe kill him, but this hurt like hell and stopped him from inhaling or exhaling for a little while. Bobby V pivoted hard on his back leg and buried his fist in the guy's liver. The big man was done. We caught him under both arms before he fell and dragged him across the floor. Folks cleared a path, and we hauled him down the stairs and dumped him against the wall outside the club. His eyes were closed, but he managed a long, wheezing gasp.

"I'll call the cops, Bobby. Make sure he stays down."

Chapter Three

I looked into the sunroom through the small square pane of wire-reinforced glass in the door. Tully had pulled a chair close to the window in the far corner and thrown his heels up on the narrow ledge, his soles pressed hard against the iron mesh. In my narrow field of vision, I could see one other person in the room, an older guy, maybe fifty or fifty-five, shuffling cards at a small table not far from where Tully looked out the window. I pushed through the door, and he looked over and was on his feet before I was fully in the room. His chair started to tip back, but he caught it without looking and set it down. He was across the room in three long strides and hugged me hard before he pushed me back to arm's length.

"E! How are you doing, man! Good to see you."

He stopped, his eyes scanning my face.

"What's going on? You look like shit."

He grabbed my arm and pulled me behind him—an orderly sat in one of the two overstuffed easy chairs in the corner.

"Jimmy. Do you mind? Me and my buddy have to chat. Privately."

The orderly looked at Tully, then gathered up the paper tented across the arm of the chair.

"Sure, Troy."

I hadn't seen the orderly before—but they came and went here. This one was a big guy, late forties with a bit of a gut, but he carried himself easy. He moved across the room, stopping to say a quiet word to the card player. I tilted my head at him. Tully shrugged.

"He's alright. Been here a couple of weeks. Seems like a good guy. So, what's going on?"

Tully, Troy Fotoula, was a large man, six-three, six-four, wide but not thick, dark-skinned with a nose that had started out prominent and been broken a couple of times -it looked more geological than biological, carved by time, tremor and shifting granite rather than a Greek father, an Italian mother and a hard overhand right after a Sleater-Kinney's show at CB's. He had shaved his head almost to the wood.

"What's with the hair?"

He ran his hand across his head and drifted. His eyes slid to the high corner of the room, flickered, wavered, and I thought he might be gone, caught in a neural riptide, pulled deep and tumbled, ragged and bagged and buried where the water meets the mud. I had seen it before. Sometimes, it was days before he floated to the surface. But he pulled back and looked at me.

"Fucking benzos."

He tapped hard on the arm of the chair. I snapped my fingers.

"Tully. The hair."

" Summer's coming. It'll be cooler. But enough bullshit, E, what's going on?"

"Looks good. Like seven kinds of whup-ass. Make everybody a little nervous, keep them on their toes?"

He grinned, tugging at the soul patch under his lip.

"It is kind of badass, isn't it? I was going to leave a strip down the middle, De Niro in Cab Driver, but that seemed a little on the nose. Got it to Brad Pitt in Fight Club and kept going."

We had known each other since we were kids, same group homes in between foster families. His folks had died in a car accident when he was eleven, and he had drifted through the system until he was eighteen, and they cut him loose.

"So, you're taking your meds, Tully?"

He nodded, quick and hard.

"This ain't about me, E. What's going on? How's Dash?

Jesus, he was good. I looked away, over his shoulder to where he had been sitting, the orange plastic chair, a little askew now.

"E—what the fuck? What happened to Dash?"

He had met her a couple of times, but they had hit it off—no surprise there—she was almost as smart as him and a little crazier. I shook my head.

"What?? What does that mean, E???"

"She's dead, Tully."

"Aw fuck. How, E.? What happened? OD?"

I shook my head again.

"Shot. Somebody took her out."

He slumped back in his chair. I hadn't noticed the ash-gray smudges under his eyes when I had come in, but now they showed on his face, pain-faded, the skin pulled tight as sucked cellophane.

"You sleeping, buddy?"

He shrugged.

"When I can."

"When was the last time?"

"A couple of days ago. Who did it?"

He had started showing signs by the time he was fifteen—missing school—not that it mattered, he was an A student whether he attended class or not—awake for days on nothing but Frosted Flakes and Mountain Dew, crazy plans for both of us—hack into the city computer system, shut down the subway and make money rickshawing people around town. Then crashing, holing up in bed for days at a time.

"You can't do this, Tully. You need to take care of yourself; you can't add any weight."

"Who did it, E?"

"I don't know. The cops are pretty sure it was me."

"You?"

He had moved forward and now sat back again, one knee shaking quick and steady.

"Makes sense, I guess. You, the boyfriend and all. They're bound to start with…"

"Ex."

"What?"

"Ex-"

"Awww. Really, E.? What happened?"

"You met her, Tully. What did you figure my shelf life was?"

He nodded.

"Yeah. You were on borrowed time. Great girl—but not up for extra innings."

I looked at him, and he shrugged his shoulders.

"Hey, you don't need me to tell you what was happening there—sometimes you get to the horn, sometimes you don't, you know that. Where are the cops on this now?"

"Who knows. But it's not your problem."

He didn't say anything and curled his fingers—bring it to me. He was my best friend. I told him the story.

* * *

"What do you think?"

Now that it was out, I wanted his take. He was the smartest guy I had ever known. He rubbed at the bridge of his nose, then pulled at the scrap of hair under his lip.

"I don't know, E. It's going to be sex or money—it always is. Maybe, your guy at the bar…but the list of guys she's dumped is pretty long—wouldn't have to be him."

He gave me a quick look.

"Sorry, pal."

I waved it off.

"But he's as good a place to start as any. How are you going to find him?"

"I figure it's Thomas Perry or the company card—he didn't look like an Antonio. I was going to start with the phone book."

"Yeah, that won't work. Nobody under forty's in the book anymore."

He was right. The guy was over forty…but trying to stay hip.

"Any suggestions?"

"Did you hear anybody talk to him?"

"What?"

"He was at the bar all night—did you hear anybody talk to him…call him by name? Maybe Dasha? The bartender?"

I hadn't thought about that. I played it back in my head. I hadn't been able to stop watching the two of them. They had stood at the end of the bar leaning in close to talk and touch, him drinking faster than her. He had gone by once on the way to the men's room and hard-eyed me. I had looked away to the end of the bar and Dasha was watching. She smiled at me and toodle-ooed her fingertips. That would be all Dasha—small, sharp cuts in a small room until we caught the blood scent.

He had argued about the bill, and I had come over when it got loud. He had ignored me when I spoke, three times, and when I put my hand on his arm, he swung on me. The kind of guy who thought he was being tricky, that swinging without talking would catch me by surprise… but I had seen the hunch in his shoulders, and it had been a long loop. By the time it reached where I was standing, I had stepped back. I raised a warning finger, but he came back with a straight right—not bad, spent a little time on a heavy bag. I tapped it past my shoulder and popped him with a hard left. Dasha had called out something. I couldn't remember what it was, but it hadn't been Tom or Thomas.

Tully nodded at the story.

"So, start with Benoit."

I nodded.

"I could sit on the address—see if the guy shows up."

Tully made a face.

"Sure…if you want to try something that will take a long time and not work. Or you could take a look at their website—maybe you get lucky and there's a picture. If not, go back to the credit card slip. Maybe he'll have a clean signature."

We didn't say anything for a few seconds.

"How are you doing?"

Tully looked around the room, then down at his leg pumping. He put his hand down to still it, but when he pulled his hand away, it started again. The big orderly looked up from the paper, watched for a second before he looked back at the paper.

"Okay. Wish I could get out."

"You sure?"

It was like I had slapped him. His head flicked back, and color rose high on his cheeks.

He stood up, and the big chair scraped across the floor. The orderly put down his paper but stayed where he was sitting. Tully walked across to the room to the orange plastic chair and dropped into it, slapping his feet up onto the ledge in the same position he had been in when I had arrived. I walked over and crouched down beside him, my bum knee protesting.

"I'm sorry, Tully. I didn't mean it like that."

He kept looking out the window. I pulled over a chair and sat with him, but we didn't speak again, and after a half hour, I left. He didn't answer when I said goodbye.

Chapter Four

"Freddie?"

He had a cell phone against his ear, but he waved me in and pointed at the chair across from his desk. Same beret, different neck scarf.

"We can go forty-five hundred dollars a night for two nights but not…"

Freddie pulled the phone away from his ear and held it up so I could hear the shouting, and pretended to spit on it, grinning at me. He put it back to his ear, waving at the chair again. I sat down. He listened.

"Listen, muchacho, I understand that they're going to be big, but we pay for big when their big—we're not talking Julión Alvarez here. Look, we can do five bills a night, but that's it. We've got to make some money here."

He listened for a moment, nodding.

"That's great, Luis. It'll be one of those two weeks in August—find out what works for your boys."

He flipped the phone shut.

"Fucking cholos—every fucking phone call's a hostage negotiation."

"Freddie, I should have asked last time, but I didn't think of it—can I get a look at the slip the guy signed, the Benoit guy that was with Dasha?"

"You're killing me here, Ones. I'm not allowed to let people flip through the credit slips."

"I don't need to see a bunch of slips, Freddie—just that one slip. See if I can make out the name."

He frowned, shook his head, and had to re-adjust the beret.

"I don't think I can do that—there are confidentiality issues that I can't ignore. I'm sorry, Einstein..."

"Freddie, it's not a big deal, just let me..."

He laughed leaned across the desk and slapped me lightly on the cheek.

"I'm busting your balls, Ones."

He reached into his shirt pocket and pulled out a slip.

"I'm way ahead of you. After you left, I figured you would end up wanting to see the signature and pulled the slip."

He put it on the desk and turned it so it was facing me. It wasn't great, but it wasn't bad either. Looked like a couple of initials to start—a B and an M or maybe a B and an N. and four letters, Stin or maybe Stan followed by a trailing line.

"What do you think? Stanley? Stanfield?"

I nodded. Freddie was seeing 'Stan.' It still looked to me like it could be "Stin."

"Thanks, Freddie. This is a big help."

Freddie pulled the slip back, waving his hand at the same time...

"Least I could do, Einstein. Dasha was a good girl."

Good girl. Didn't know about that. But she was something.

I was on the top step when he stopped me.

"If this turns out to be the guy...if you're sure this is the guy, I mean, without a single fragment of a doubt sure he's the guy...you come talk to me."

It was his voice coming from behind me, but I could imagine his face, set and hard. He liked to play the gruff, congenial bar owner, but he was a hard guy, and he knew some people. Guys that went right in didn't take a number.

"Sure, Freddie. Thanks."

But I wasn't sure I would be able to cross that line.

* * *

Benoit Assets had offices in a high rise on the corner of East Fifty-Fifth and Madison. It was a long way up. I tried to count to the thirty-fourth floor but lost it where the early morning sun splashed against the mirrored glass. I had gone to their website but there were no photographs of employees—not even the top management staff. But there was a Robert Stinson. He was one of six senior portfolio managers. Sounded like money. It figured that a guy like that would be at work early.

I didn't have the wardrobe to pass myself off as a money manager, so I went with the bicycle delivery look—baggy shorts, t-shirt, company-mandated helmet in hand but wearing a flip-bill ballcap, mailbag with a cross-the-chest bandolier-style strap. They didn't even call up, just made me sign in—I went with Henry Gondorff...Paul was badass in that film. It was easier than I expected—the receptionist wasn't on the desk yet, but the glass doors were unlocked.

Benoit wasn't a huge company—they had the south side of the floor... some property management company had the other side. There was a framed chart on the wall behind the receptionist's desk with room numbers, and Stinson was in 3417.

I guessed wrong, had to double back past the receptionist's desk and found Stinson's office in the back corner. The door was closed, but I got lucky; it was unlocked and led right into his main office—it didn't look like anybody got their own secretary. But this was high-end, floor-to-ceiling windows on two walls, plush white carpet, a black desk with the computer keyboard built in, and two side-by-side screens attached in the middle of the desk and work spaces to the right and left of the screens. It looked like the desk was mounted on hydraulics so that Stinson could work standing up if he wanted. There was a sixty-inch flat screen mounted on the wall facing the desk, black and silent now but likely scrolling Bloomberg during the day. A picture of him, his wife, and two daughters, the girls and Mom, all blondes, on the right-hand side of the desk. The girls looked about six and eight years old. His wife was hot—okay, on the far side of hot, starting to cool but still hot. It was him.

I sat in the chair, but the raised desk blocked my view of the door. And it would block his view of me in his chair. It took a few minutes to figure out the desk, and I kept my eye on the door while I played with the buttons. The gears and machining hardly made a sound as the desk rose and fell. I lowered it until it clunked softly and stopped and sat down again to check the sight lines. It worked—when he stepped in, all he had to do was glance at his desk, and he would see me. Yeah. It's me—it turns out I have a season's pass to beat your ass.

Who says that shit? Focus.

My stomach was churning now. It was always the same—I was OK when I was jacked up and moving, but once I had a little time, these things always seemed like they might be a bad idea. There wasn't once I hadn't settled into the chute, felt the twelve hundred pounds of bone and gristle underneath me, wound the bull rope, and wondered what the hell I was doing.

For the first five minutes I stared at the door waiting for the handle to turn and for the next ten I spun the chair, switching between looking through a gap in a couple of taller buildings across the East River to Brooklyn and watching the door. The fifteen minutes after that I spent looking for the remote for the big screen—it would be set to Bloomberg, but it could probably get other channels. I finally found it in a narrow compartment on the underside of the desk and flipped to a sports channel looping through last night's highlights. The Royals had beat the Yankees on a one-hitter by Santana—the kid reminded me of Saberhagen—tweezer-thin and a ghost pepper fastball.

I waited another ten, went to the door, and stuck my head out—Stinson was five strides away and looking at me. I pulled my head back and closed the door. I waited two beats—yeah, me holed up in the office wasn't a good plan—and stuck my head out again. He was standing in the same place. His face looked good—like I had never hit him. I was surprised by how much that disappointed me.

"Who are you?"

Not bad. Pretty steady. Like there was a chance he was still in charge.

"Mr. Stinson. Why don't you step into your office? We should talk."

"Who are you, and what are you doing in my office?"

He hadn't recognized me yet. I figured there was a reasonably good chance I could grab him and shove him into the office before he could react. But if I couldn't, and things went south, I was likely looking at assault, trespassing, or maybe kidnapping. Didn't matter. It was too late. He was walking away.

"I'm getting security."

I stepped into the hallway.

"Whoa, Bobby. It's about Dasha."

That stopped him...like I had fired a warning shot over his head. His shoulders hunched, and his knees buckled a little. He spoke without turning.

"What about Dasha?"

"We should talk in private."

I didn't wait. I went back into his office, around his desk, and sat down in his chair. Not exactly like I planned it but still—it put me in his chair when he walked in the door. It took him so long to get to the door that I thought I might have miscalculated, but as I was starting to get back up again, he edged into the doorway. The guy was screwing with my timing—half up out of the chair was not the look I was going for. I sat back down again and waved him in.

"C'mon, Bob. Nothing to worry about—I just want to talk."

He looked to his right up the hallway, and I knew he was replaying it in his mind. How thirty seconds earlier, he was a guy with a beautiful wife and two beautiful kids and a great job with a beautiful view—beautiful, beautiful, beautiful—and now he was going to get bent over his desk by a guy in a flipped-up Peugeot cap. He was trying to figure out how to reel it back in. I waved again.

'It's too late, Bobby. We're going to have a chat—there's no way around that. So, come in, close the door behind you, and let's talk."

He thought for a second but did it. I waved at a chair against the wall.

"Sit down. This may take a few minutes."

"What about Dasha? Did she send you?"

"When did you see her last, Bobby?"

He started to answer but stopped.

"Do I know you? Have we met?"

"You're a quick healer, Bobby. What's it been—two and a half weeks? You wouldn't even know I had popped you."

He got it and reached behind for the handle of the door without taking his eyes off me—watching his fear calmed me down. It was so freaking primal—pre-dated tooth and claw. The tough guys could inhale it quick, pull it back under the skin, so you weren't sure you had even seen it, but not this guy; it crawled around his face like ants on a banana skin.

"Don't do that, Bob. We still have Dasha to talk about. That hasn't changed. You make a big fuss, everybody's going to know about Dasha."

I pointed at the picture.

"Your wife, your daughters."

His hand stayed on the handle for a long second, then dropped back to his side.

"What do you want?"

"Dasha."

"What about Dasha?"

"When did you see her last?"

"About a week after the night in the bar."

"She dump you?"

He looked startled.

"Dump me? No, we had dinner, went back to her place. I left about one AM. She said she was going to be busy for a few days but that she would call me. "

"Did she?"

His face fell a little, even afraid; he was feeling this one. I liked him a little better.

"No. I haven't heard from her since—almost two weeks."

You could never be absolutely sure, but I couldn't see the lie on his face.

"What did she say she was going to be doing for those few days?"

He shook his head.

"She didn't say."

He looked at me. I raised an eyebrow, but he shrugged.

"You know Dasha. She tells what she wants to tell. When I asked her what was happening she laughed and told me to mind my own business."

He was right; that sounded like Dasha—like trying to ladle smoke into a soup bowl.

"What did you think was going on?"

He shrugged again.

"No idea. She doesn't share much."

"Drugs?"

He pointed at a chair facing his desk, and I nodded, so he sat down, looking to his left out the window. I could see I had lost him.

"Bobby, c'mon—keep your head in the game. Do you think drugs were in play?"

It took a second, but he looked at me.

"Drugs? Could be, I guess. She always had a little weed. Coke for special occasions. But no more than usual."

"Was anything different?"

He was looking out the window again, and when he spoke, it wasn't an answer.

"I don't understand why you're here. I don't understand the questions. Jealous ex-boyfriend? Is that it? Coming here to tell me to lay off Dasha? To move along?"

He looked at me, holding my eyes. He was touching bottom, catching his balance, the slack coming out of his face and the shake out of his voice.

"Haven't you figured it out yet…that you're still a step behind? That, I'm her latest ex. I didn't have it figured out until now, but you've been on this for a while. You should be talking to the next guy."

Just enough confidence coming back to bring the asshole to the surface. It pissed me off.

"She's dead, Bobby—two to the back of the head. But make no mistake—she dumped you. There's no way she was going to stay with a guy who got stopped by a straight jab."

I stood up and walked past him out of the office. I should have asked a couple more questions, but some lines were for leaving.

Chapter Five

I could see that he was on the downside. It was only two days, but he was down to grey ash, with no heat or light. I pushed through the door, walked across the room and sat down beside him. He didn't even look over. There was a different orderly sitting in the corner.

"Hey, Tully."

It took a couple of seconds.

"E."

We sat for several minutes without talking.

"Sorry about last time, E."

"My fault, Tools. Sometimes I say dumb shit."

His mouth curled a little at one side, more grimace than smile.

"Nah. You had it right. Don't know what I was thinking."

I let that go.

"I found the guy."

"Yeah?"

"You had it right—matched the name on the credit card with a name on the website, had a chat with him."

"And?"

He spoke without looking over. I couldn't tell if he was really curious or going along.

"He didn't seem right for it. Didn't seem like he knew she was dead."

"Yeah. Well. You wouldn't be that hard to fool."
I looked over.
"You still pissed?"
The corner of the eye I could see creased slightly.
"Maybe a little."
"We gonna' be okay?"
"Always."
He was right about that.

* * *

Tully had stepped into the lunchroom like a fawn stepping out of the trees—there were two six-seater tables, and the empty seat was across from me. Nevy had got caught creeping some old couple's house one block over and sent to juvie. When the cops showed up, he was sitting in the dark watching the Disney channel and eating leftover lasagna from the old folk's fridge. He was a fuckup but not a bad guy.

"Hi."
It caught me by surprise—most guys keep their head down or come at you hard.
"My name's Troy."
I looked at him.
"Fatoula. People call me Tully."
He stretched his hand across the table, tapped the edge of his milk glass but caught it before it could spill then left his hand out. I looked, hoping he would put it away, but he didn't so I shook it.
"Einstein."
"What?"
"His name's fucking Einstein, fuckee. What don't you get?"
Frank Spitz. He was the oldest and biggest guy in the house—fourteen years old and a smidge over six feet. I had been here a couple of months,

but it didn't take long to figure out the setup. There was Frank and his posse, a couple of Anglo kids that had been in the system for years, and a Hispanic kid who didn't say much but tagged along wherever the three of them went. They ran the place. Most of the time, you were OK if you kept your head down and stayed out of their way.

Tully looked over at Spitz, his face clear and open.

Oh. Einstein. Right. Got it."

"Right. Got it."

In a high, girlish voice. Tully ignored it and bit into his sandwich.

"Look at me, fuckwad."

"Knock it off, Spitz."

Harold, one of the house councilors, had stepped into the room. Spitz had started to stand but sat back down, still glaring at Tully. Tully kept his eyes on the table and took another bite of his sandwich, the red rising from his collar into his cheeks.

* * *

Nevy had been my roommate so now Tully was—he had the bed on the other side of the room. It was quiet time after clearing up the lunch dishes. Everybody spent time in their room—the intention was for studying or reading, but most guys were on their Gameboys. Tully didn't stop talking. Both his parents had died in a car accident. It had been six weeks. Neither of his parents had family that could take him. Tully's dad had been a civil engineer, an only child and both of his parents had died when he was in his twenties. His Mom was a dentist with a younger sister who had Down's. Tully's grandmother had died of breast cancer two years before, and his grandfather had early-stage Alzheimer's.

That explained a lot. He was from a whole different world. The rest of us were veterans of the system—he had no clue.

My own story was the usual one—I had no idea who my father was, and my mom was a junkie. She hadn't given me up—I'll give her that. Child services had come and taken me away when I was two years old. There had been a short stint when I was four where my Mom had cleaned up enough to get me back, but it hadn't lasted long. By that time, adoption was a long shot, and I had drifted between short-term foster homes and group homes ever since.

Tully and I had nothing in common, but I kind of liked him. Tully was twelve. I was eleven.

* * *

"They'll likely come tonight."

"Who?"

"Frankie and those other three assholes."

"Why?"

"He doesn't like you."

"Why not?"

"He doesn't like anybody."

"What will he do?"

I looked over at him to see if he was kidding.

"Kick your ass. Maybe mine, too."

"What did I do?"

I shrugged.

"Nothing. You're a new guy."

"What are we going to do? Can we talk to somebody?"

Talk to somebody. It had never occurred to me. I shook my head.

"Nah. Nobody to talk to. What would we tell them? Try and get your licks in."

We didn't talk for a few seconds.

"My Dad said that there's never a need to resort to physical violence."

I laughed.

* * *

They didn't come that night. They came the second night. I didn't wake up until I heard Tully cry out. They were gray shadows, and they punched him as he lay in the bed. I wished that I could stay in bed, pretend that I was asleep. Somebody must have covered his mouth because the noises Tully made were harsh and hoarse but muffled as if they came from behind a closed door. I swung my legs over the side of the cot, but nobody noticed. I sat for another second, thinking they might stop and leave, but they didn't and I pushed off hard, driving into the nearest shadow. I was small for my age but wound tight and sprung easy. Whoever it was, I caught them in the soft spot above the hipbone and drove them across Tully's cot into the wall. He hit hard, and it sounded loud in the room. It was confusion as they scrambled for the door. The guy I had tackled pushed me off, and in seconds, the room was empty, and there was just me sprawled across the foot of Tully's cot. I slipped back to my cot before the door opened, and light splashed into the room. It was Randi, one of the overnight councilors.

"You guys okay? I heard a bang."

We're good—I tripped on something."

"That you, Einstein?"

"Yeah."

"How's the new guy?"

"He's good."

"OK. Keep it quiet now."

She closed the door behind her. We didn't speak for a long while, and I thought that he might be asleep.

"Will they come back?"

"Not tonight."

* * *

I didn't get my first look at Tully until breakfast—he was already up and out when I woke up. They had worked him over pretty good. He must have turned to the side because there were a couple of welts, both on the left side of his face and a gash over his left eye that had scabbed over, rust-brown. Harold noticed when he came into the room.

"What happened to you, Troy?"

Tully looked at him, then at me. I shook my head. But his jaw set and his eyes narrowed—it would be an expression I would come to know well, and he pointed across the table at Spitz.

"This guy and his three buddies came into our room last night."

He pointed at his face.

"They did this."

He stood and raised his shirt. It was worse there.

"And this."

Harold looked at me.

"Flint?"

I looked at the plate and up at Harold, then around the table before settling on Tully. I was boxed in tight.

"Yeah. That sounds about right."

"That's bullshit. They're lying."

Harold looked at Spitz.

"So, how did this happen, Spitz? Falling out of bed?"

* * *

"That was stupid, Tully."

"What was stupid?"

But he knew what I meant. We were back in our room, both sprawled on our cots, staring at the ceiling.

"What was I supposed to do? Say nothing happened?"

"They can't help you, Tully…the councilors? They got nothing. Some of them are OK, but they can't watch you all the time. This is ours."

"What do we do?"

"Stick together. Ride it out."

He swung his legs off the cot and sat up.

"That's crazy. There has to be somebody who can help us."

I didn't answer. He would have to figure it out.

* * *

Spitz wouldn't get a chance at the house for a while, but he came at me at school. I had known it was coming. He couldn't let it hang that I had stepped in and then ratted him out.

I saw him coming from across the yard—him and two of his boys—lay the book, Max Brand, spine-split in the dirt and pushed off the chain-link fence to my feet. He had a foot or better on me, and the other two, though shorter than Spitz, were still a lot bigger than me.

"Tully."

He was still reading, not seeing it coming.

"What?"

He looked at me, then across the playground.

"Oh."

He stood up.

"I got Spitz."

"What?"

My only chance was knowing that the fight had started before they did. I set my foot against the fence behind me, and when they were close, I pushed off and drove my shoulder into his gut. He wasn't expecting it, and I heard the wind come out of him as he sat down hard and tipped back so his head smacked into the dirt. I scrambled up onto his chest and got two punches in before he bucked me off. After that, it was a beating, ten or twelve hard shots before the shouting brought teachers over to break it up. They didn't all hit flush, but I was bleeding from my nose and a split over my left eye, and when I stood up, the ground tilted under me, and I almost went down again. Tully hadn't moved from his spot against the fence.

* * *

I lay on my cot, staring at the ceiling. I wished I could close my eyes and sleep, but every time I did, the room spun, and I thought I might puke. My face was lumped and sore where Spitz had hit me, and my left hip ached where I had been kicked when I was on the ground. I hadn't noticed then, but it hurt now.

"My dad said that it doesn't make sense to meet violence with violence."

I didn't answer.

"He said that most things can be talked out. That there should never be a need for violence."

I could see where somebody had killed a mosquito against the ceiling, leaving a thin grey smear. Maybe leaving it there would keep other mosquitos away, a warning.

"He said that individuals should never resort to violence…that things can almost always be worked out, and if they can't, you bring in the authorities. You don't take things into your own hands."

I wished I could turn to face the wall, but my sore hip wouldn't allow it.

"No offence, Tully, but what the fuck did your dad know?"

* * *

They came the next day, again. Tully was in the same spot as the day before, but I had moved away to the other corner of the playground. I had finished 'Three on the Trail' and moved on to 'Smiling Charlie.' They started towards me but spotted Tully and shifted direction. He didn't notice them until they stopped in a tight, close circle. He scrambled to his feet and tried to smile but it wouldn't hold, sagging and twitching like he was popping stitches, finding temporary purchase but sliding loose until he gave up and let it fall. He took the first couple of shots standing and was still up by the time I caught Spitz with an overhand right behind the ear. He didn't see it coming, and it felt good. Didn't put him down, though, and they buried us.

* * *

Five of us sat outside the nurse's office—the sixth, one of Spitz's boys, was in getting patched up. Me and Tully were banged up good—I was bleeding from at least three different spots on my face, and he was going to need stitches under one eye—but Spitz and the other two were a little dinged up, too. These two weren't bleeding, but Spitz's ear on the side where I had hit him was puffed and misshapen, and the shorter, dark-haired one had red blotches where somebody had caught him…might have been me, but I couldn't remember. The pudgy redhead who was in with the nurse had thrown up, so they were checking for concussion.

"You're dead now, motherfucker."

I stared at my hands, trying to keep them still.

"You hear me?"

I kept my head down. Nothing I could say here changed anything. You were either ready to go, or you weren't.

"Why did you help me out?"

That one caught me by surprise, and I almost looked up but caught myself. He asked again.

"I didn't help you. Why did you help me?"

I stared at my hands for a few seconds before the door to the nurse's office opened, and she let that ginger prick out and called my name. I walked in without looking at any of them.

*　*　*

"Why, Einstein?"

We were lying on the cots again. The school had reported back to the home, and the six of us were confined to our rooms for the weekend. At least it postponed the next beating.

"Why did you help me out? You didn't owe me anything."

He had asked it at least ten times now. He was starting to get on my nerves.

"Shut up."

I should have known it was a mistake—it only encouraged him.

"Why would you help me? I didn't deserve it. I stood and watched them beat the shit out of you."

Tully said 'shit' like he hadn't very often. I shifted on the cot, trying to find a position that was comfortable, but they had worked me over pretty good, and it was tough to find a spot. It was hard not to think about Monday. I was pretty sure they were just getting started. Maybe they would transfer us out if it got too bad—put us in another school. How bad did it have to get before they moved you out? Or maybe never. Maybe it went on and on, and it didn't matter that you couldn't take it anymore because you took it anyway. Taking was all there was.

"Why, Einstein? Why did you help me?"

It had grown dark while we were lying there, and maybe the grey and shade made it tougher to stay quiet.

"It's not about you."

A car drove by, and the headlights washed across the walls and were gone, and the gloom settled like dust. I sat up on the edge of the cot, pushed myself to my feet, and the pain in my side and hip wobbled me. I moved across to the wall beside the door and ran my fingers across the paint until I felt the depression I had spotted when the car lights had lit the room. It was a nail hole. Someone had hung something here, a painting or a photograph, but I couldn't think of what it would be. I couldn't imagine it.

"What are you doing?"

He spoke quietly, but it sounded loud in the room. I moved back and lowered myself slowly onto the cot.

"You think I give a shit about you?"

"This has nothing to do with you."

"It's about me."

"Fuck, what if I don't help you? What does that make me?"

"One of the bad guys. "

"One of the fucking bad guys. "

"No fucking way. "

"No fucking way, I'm one of the bad guys."

Fuck. I could feel them coming, but I couldn't stop now.

"I'm a good guy. A good fucking guy. Stand-up. They come at you; I'll be standing even if you're not. You or anybody else."

I was crying now. Crying hard, but I couldn't stop talking.

"And one time, one fucking time, I won't be standing alone. There'll be somebody else standing up. Back to back. Some tough motherfucker that won't back down no matter how bad it gets, and they can beat me broken, beat me busted, beat me blind and silent, beat me so I don't know my name or place or how I got to here and me and him will stand back to back against it all. In the dark, in the light, in the rain and wind, and when it's too fucking hot to breathe, we'll stand. We'll stand. We'll fucking stand."

The words came out hitching and wet, and I stopped, too embarrassed even to swipe at the snot under my nose.

"Fuck."

I think Tully fell asleep before I did.

*　*　*

They came on Monday at the first recess. I thought they might wait, let things die down a little. A third fight in less than a week meant a suspension for sure. But they didn't care about that. I knew they wouldn't, but it hadn't stopped me from hoping. Tully was sitting at the other end of the fence. He hadn't tried to talk to me the rest of the weekend nor on the bus to school, nor while we read, leaning back against the fence. He had taken a spot well down the fence, maybe hoping to stay out of harm's way. It might work for a while but once they were through with me they would get to him, he hadn't figured it out.

I hadn't been reading—couldn't keep my mind on it…kept reading the same words over again—because I was keeping my eye on the yard watching for Spitz. It hadn't taken long. I stood up and slid the book into my back pocket. This was going to be a bad one, and I didn't want the book lying forgotten in the dirt—the Sackett Brand…it had taken me a while to track it down, and I didn't want it going missing. The pain was fresh enough that my stomach flipped, and I could feel the tremble beginning. I let it build, waiting for it to flip and shift, fear to rage, getting me through the next few minutes without pissing myself. The grin on Spitz's face as he moved across the grass a step ahead of his boys and his ear looking fine took me the rest of the way, and I stepped forward knowing my shots would come early or not at all.

Tully caught my arm.

"Not yet. Take this."

He must have been watching and spotted them at the same time I had. And he had come more prepared than me. He held out a fist-sized piece of rust-red brick in his left hand. He had another in his right. I took it, hefted it—it was too big for my hand, the broken edges scraping my palm and fingers.

"Is it OK if we keep the fence at our back?"

"What?"

"Do we have to stand back to back?"

I looked at him for a second and turned to Spitz. They had stopped a couple of steps away from us when they saw the bricks. Tully started talking.

"We will brick you. We will brick you in the face and in the stomach and in the arms. I swear to God we will bri…"

Tully was still learning. I stepped in and hit Spitz in the forehead, and something gave—in the brick and beneath the skin. He dropped like slopped water, hitting the ground before the dusting and shards from the edge of the brick did.

I'll give Tully credit—it stopped him, but not for long. He looked down at Spitz, prone but not still, twitching like a hooked fish on the dock, his eyes ratcheted back beneath his lids so that only the whites showed, blood seeping from a gash over his left eye, the swelling already distorting his face, then he looked at the other three. They were already watching Tully, and when he stepped forward, the brick not even raised, hanging easy in his hand by his side, they ran.

Me and Tully.

* * *

He sat slumped in his chair, now staring out the window.

"I've got to go, Tools."

I couldn't tell if he heard me.

Chapter Six

They grabbed me up outside of Boom Boom's—same two guys—and made me sit for an hour looking at the walls. Same room, same scuffed paint job, same smell of stale body odor and cigarette smoke.

I looked around for the microphone in the room but couldn't see it. Maybe in the sprinkler head. Should call a lawyer, but I didn't know any…and they cost money I didn't want to spend.

There were two possibilities—either Stinson had made a complaint, or something had come up with Dasha.

"C'mon boys, let's do this. You got questions, ask them. I was supposed to be on the door half an hour ago."

I felt like an ass talking to an empty room. Ten more minutes passed. Nothing. What the hell? I stood up and walked across the room to the door. As I put my hand out to grab the handle, the door pushed open and I had to take a step back. Then another. Both detectives pushed through the door, the older black cop first.

"Going somewhere, Einstein?"

"You know it's my first name, don't you officer?"

"What?"

"You keep saying it hard, as if it's my last name. But it ends up sounding kind of friendly…like were buddies. And I don't even know your name."

The other cop grinned large, not trying to hide it.

"Detectives Evans and Dwight. Grab a seat, Mr. Flint."

"You've got something new on Dasha?"

"Grab a seat, and we can chat about what we've got."

"I'm late for work already."

"This shouldn't take long, Mr. Flint."

I sat down again, and Evans sat across from me with his back to the door. Dwight leaned against the back wall, arms folded, watching expressionless. Evans made a show of flipping through some sheets he had in a folder in front of him.

"Any new ideas about what might have happened to Dasha, Mr. Flint?"

He asked it without looking up from the sheets, but I was pretty sure he wasn't reading anything. I wondered again if Stinson had made a complaint. But this didn't seem like the way they would approach a formal complaint.

"Really, Detective Evans? You've brought me in here to ask me if there's anything new?"

I stood up.

"Next time, phone. You've got my number."

He looked up but not startled, an easy smile on his face.

"Relax, Mr. Flint. Please sit down. You know there's more to it than that. We like to start out slow."

I sat back down. I wanted to know what was going on. Evans looked back at his notes.

"One theory is that she was mixed up with drugs and got into trouble with a supplier."

I hesitated, wondering what I should tell them, but it hit me again… that she was dead—she couldn't get in worse trouble than she was in. It was sharper and heavier every time it hit.

"Dasha liked drugs, Detective Evans, and she sold a little—but small time. She didn't deal with any of the heavy hitters."

"Heavy hitters? Like who?"

This from Dwight against the wall. I couldn't tell if the interruption bothered Evans.

"I wouldn't know."

"But you said heavy hitters like you did know."

He had me there. I didn't know names, but there were a couple of guys that came in Sundays and Mondays that had the reputation. Sinaloa guys. Sicario's. You left them alone, let them drink, and walk on their tab if they forgot to pay. They tipped big, and if you had to cover their bill once in a while, so be it.

"You know the bar business. You hear things. Dasha never had anything to do with the heavies."

"But you'd know the guys. Know who you needed to go to if you needed work done?"

I stared at Evans when I answered.

"You still banging that drum, Detective Dwight?"

He pushed away from the wall.

"That's the story we're hearing."

Evans tried to keep his face still, but he tightened around the lips and eyes for a flash. That stopped me. They thought they had something… and Evans was pissed that his partner had dropped it on the table so soon.

"What story's that?"

"That you had it done."

Evans had taken over again.

"Where did you hear that?"

"Talk on the street."

"Talk on the street. Right. While you're swapping swigs on a forty with your homies."

I stood up again.

"One of your boys is feeding you shit. I don't know why, but they are. I'm done here. "

"Sit down, Mr. Flint."

"Am I under arrest?"

Evans swiveled in his chair, looked at his partner, and turned back to me.

"No, you're no…"

"Then I'm done."

I went to the door and pulled on the handle, expecting it to be locked, but the door opened, and I walked out. They didn't stop me.

Chapter Seven

I met Dasha my first night at Boom Boom's. She was still working the bar for Frankie. Cutoff jean shorts, cowboy boots, checked shirt tied off beneath her breasts so lots of flat belly showed—topped with a straw Stetson that would have looked like a joke on most women. The late-night crowd loved her—she could dance Norteña better than any Mexican I had ever seen, and she did every night. The regulars knew and would start calling for her as it got late. She would completely ignore them until she didn't, that moment when she would come out from behind the bar and push through the crowd to the dance floor. On the way, she would be scouting the crowd, and by the time she made it to the floor, she would have found her guy, whether he was with somebody or not. She would point and curl her finger. She would fit herself to the guy, tongue and groove, like for those few minutes they were two heads on a single body. Nobody ever turned her down.

Now I sat at the bar waiting for Freddy to finish up. He had asked to see me.

"Did he say what he wanted, Mikey?"

"He didn't say, Ones. Just told me that if you showed up to get you to hang around."

I nodded. It was late, and I was tired, but maybe Freddie had some information I could use. Plus, he was the boss. He slipped up beside me at the bar.

"Ones."

"Hey, Freddie."

"What happened tonight?"

"Cops pulled me in. I'm still their guy."

"Fuckers. You need a lawyer?"

"I don't think so. Not yet, anyway."

"I can get you a lawyer. I know some good lawyers."

"Thanks, Freddie. If it gets to there, I may take you up on it."

I wouldn't, but it didn't seem polite to say that. We sat for a couple of minutes without talking until I couldn't help myself.

"You wanted to see me, Freddie?"

He didn't answer right away, and I pushed the beer sweat around the bar with the bottom of my bottle, then looked over. Freddie rubbed at the side of his left eye, pushing at a pale scar outside his eyebrow, not looking at me.

"I know this is a bad time for you, Ones."

He scratched at something on the bar until it flicked free.

"Dasha and everything."

Jesus Christ. These guys that couldn't leave the obvious unsaid.

"But I need you on the door. I need to know that if you're on the schedule, you'll show up."

"Are you firing me, Freddie?"

He looked over.

"Fire you! No. Fuck, no. Jesus Christ, Ones, what are you thinking? Fuck, how do you think I would do that? No. I'm saying that I need you here and on the job. Maybe it makes sense to take me up on the lawyer, so you don't have to handle this on your own. You can piece some of this off to somebody that does it for a living,"

It was my turn to look away.

"Sorry, Freddie. Didn't mean to jump on you. This one's got me twisted."

He patted my arm twice and pulled his hand away.

"I appreciate the offer, Freddie, and I may take you up on it. Just not yet."

"Good, Ones. It's an open offer—no matter what happens."

He stood up.

"I've got to get back to the books, buddy."

"Sure, Freddie. Thanks. For everything."

"No worries, Einstein. I take care of mine."

I waggled my empty beer bottle at Mikey. He came over, wiped the pale pool on the bar, and set another down before grabbing up the empty.

"Mikey, there's a guy comes in most Sundays…once in a while on Mondays. You know the guy I mean—dresses sharp…"

Mikey shook his head.

"Nah, Ones. You don't want to mix up with that guy—fucker's plugged in tight. If he's the one did Dasha…"

He shrugged.

"What are you saying, Mikey?"

"They don't fuck around, Ones. You get on the wrong side of this guy; you be grateful if they only blow your fucking head off."

"I want to talk to him, Mikey."

He was already walking away, shaking his head, but he turned around and came back and stood facing me.

"You see the fucked-up psycho comes in with him?"

"Yeah. Messed-up face—looks like it was used as a brake pad."

"Yeah. Good one, Ones. Try that out on him. He's a chuckling motherfucker."

"What's your point, Mikey?"

"It's called 'la danza de la cuerda del Diablo'—dance of the devil's rope. You heard of it?"

I shook my head.

"They wrapped him in barbwire, head to fucking toe, tied him to the bumper of a tricked-out Chevy Suburban, and drove him half a mile on a dirt road, bouncing and skidding like a hanging tailpipe. Left him for dead, but he made it to a farmhouse—dragging wire and torn meat."

I nodded.

"He looks tough."

Mikey made a face.

"Tough? You think that's what the story is about? How tough he is?"

He laughed, happy, truly amused, his teeth showing even and white against his skin.

"You fucking gringos."

He got called down the bar and ambled away to pull a beer from the fridge, then strolled back and picked up as if he hadn't left.

"He killed every one of those fuckers. Every one. Got the driver last. Mailed parts of the guy to his wife every day for a month, then left a message saying where to find what was left of the poor cocksucker. A torso and a head, still breathing—the guy lasted two more days. Never slept once and didn't make a sound—his vocal cords were shredded from screaming."

"Sounds like a story."

Mikey looked at me, then walked away. He didn't turn around this time.

* * *

The music was loud, and customers were stacked two or three deep at the bar except for the space where Raul Vargas sat. The man with the damaged face stood beside Vargas, watching the room. The place where his nose should have been, was a shapeless mound, his nostrils flush to the skin, like a second pair of dark eyes. The left side of his mouth was pulled down hard as if he was barb-hooked and reeled, and his right lid draped so that a sliver of his eye glistened beneath the puckered flesh. Scars crisscrossed his face in a way that I wouldn't have understood if I hadn't heard Mikey's story.

I hung across the bar so Mikey could see me and nodded for him to come over. He looked down the bar to where Vargas sat and back at me, shook his head, then turned back to talk to a couple of young women at the bar. I worked my way down the bar, but by the time I got there, he had found an excuse to move to the spot I had vacated. I chased him around the bar a couple of times and finally caught him serving a couple that had come in.

"Mikey, tell Vargas I want to speak to him."

"No fucking way, Ones. You wanna' jump, you go ahead…but I ain't gonna' open the window."

"C'mon Mikey. Tell him I want a word. One minute of his time."

"What are you talking to me for? I ain't his fucking road manager. Why would he listen to me?"

"Don't bullshit me, Mikey. I've seen you guys talking. He likes you. He listens to you. C'mon. You don't ask him; I'm going to go in cold."

He turned away to get drinks for a waitress, and I started to back out through the crowd. He turned and called to me over his shoulder.

"Chill would ya'…for one fucking second. I'll talk to him, alright? Give me one second."

I nodded and mouthed *thanks*, but he wasn't looking.

Mikey finished putting the drinks together and moved down the bar, ignoring a couple of customers waving at him, and leaned in to speak to Vargas. Mikey looked over at me a couple of times as they spoke, but Vargas didn't. Mikey did most of the talking, but I could see that Vargas asked a couple of questions—questions that Mikey didn't look happy to answer. Finally, he gave a short nod. Mikey worked his way back up the bar, taking a couple of orders as he went, then caught my eye and nodded.

Vargas's guy stepped forward as I came around the bar. He stepped into the space between me and Vargas and reached for my waist, but Vargas stopped him. The man stood for a moment, then stepped back when Vargas shook his head again. Vargas looked at me for a long time before speaking. When he did, his voice was soft, the accent barely detectable.

"Vicente is a suspicious man. It has saved my life several times. But sometimes, he is more cautious than is necessary."

"Caution is rarely a mistake, Mr. Vargas."

"This is true, but we must breathe, Mr. Einstein."

"Einstein, Mr. Vargas. Not Mr."

"Ah, a nickname. You must be an intelligent man."

"No, sir. It's my given name. Einstein. By my mother."

Vargas raised his eyebrows.

"Ahhh, a name to live up to. "

I nodded.

"My father named me Raul. He told me it was because it was a simple name. It held nothing. You could be anything. Nothing or everything. It was an empty glass waiting to be filled. But Einstein—this is something else, no? It is a meal already prepared—you can eat it or push away from the table, but you don't get to make your own."

"It's a name."

"And you are a bouncer?"

"That's correct, Mr. Vargas."

I watched the corners of his mouth twitch. He was having fun with me.

"So, what did you want to talk about, Mr. Flint?"

He had known my name from the moment I had stepped around the bar. Maybe before.

"A woman that used to work here. A bartender. Dasha Bragin."

I watched his face for something, anything—but the look of faint amusement didn't shift.

"The girl who was killed. Beaten and shot in the head. I heard about this. What did you want to know?"

I hesitated, embarrassed by the question I wanted to ask.

"Have you heard anything? Is there word out there about who did it?"

"Really? You want to know if I've heard anything? Did you hear Mr. Flint, Vicente? He would like me to be his informant. Keep my ear to the ground—is that how they say it, Mr. Flint?

"It's not like that, Mr. Vargas. I want to know…"

"What you want to know Mr. Flint? Einstein. Is whether we did it. Whether we killed Dasha. Whether she had somehow offended us and we had found it necessary to kill her. But you were too afraid to ask that question."

I looked at him and at his man beside him, the eyes alive and sparking in the dead, ridged skin.

"You're right. That was the question. But I wasn't too afraid. It seemed rude. I apologise. I should have asked what I wanted to know."

His face relaxed a little.

"So, you think I should tell you our business? Who we kill and who we don't? Why would I do that, Mr. Flint? Why would I speak to you of these things?"

"Because I need to know, Mr. Vargas."

"And if I killed her, Mr. Flint. If I was the one who put the gun against her head and pulled the trigger. What then?"

I stared at him. He was a handsome man. Small, symmetric features; tapered, wideset dark eyes, a thin straight nose over narrow pale lips, and square white teeth, so even, they might have been fake. He was amused by me again.

I shook my head.

"I don't know Mr. Vargas. I don't know what I would do."

"It would be interesting to find out."

Vargas turned back to the bar and I moved forward but his man stepped between us, one hand flat against my chest. I could see it in my mind, coming up hard under the arm, driving the heel of my palm into his chin, snapping his teeth together so hard that some would chip or break, using the momentum I had already built up to hammer my elbow into his throat. But I had little doubt where that would end up—me in a warehouse somewhere being pulled apart in a way that you couldn't stitch up. I backed up and felt the fingers of his hand trail off my chest, turned, and pushed through the crowd, down the stairs, and into the street. I stood sucking in air, letting the evening breeze cool my face, allowing my heart to slow.

* * *

I sat at the bar after we closed, watching Mikey clean up and stock for the next day.

"What did Vargas ask you?"

He tilted the hinged bar top up and went past me to go down to the beer room. I followed him, ducking my head to avoid the low jamb.

"Mikey?"

"If you're going to follow me around, at least grab a couple of Heinie's."

I picked up a couple of cases and followed him back up the stairs.

"Mikey?"

"He wanted to know who I was—that I thought I could schedule his meetings."

"Sorry, Mikey. I didn't mean to put you in the middle."

"Where did you think you were putting me?"

I swung the cases up on the bar, feeling it in my knee.

"Guess I wasn't thinking."

"Fucking right about that."

"Vargas pay his tab?"

"What do you think?"

I put a couple of fifties on the bar, but Mikey swatted them onto the floor.

"Fuck you."

I bent, picked up the bills and stuffed them in my pocket. He was right. Fuck me.

* * *

Frankie caught me as I was grabbing my coat to leave.

"Einstein, come here."

He patted the seat beside him at the bar.

"It's been a long night, Frankie."

"Gimme a minute. I just want to chat."

I slipped up on the stool beside him.

"What's up?"

"You were talking to Raul Vargas?"

"Yeah."

"What did you talk about?"

"No offence, Freddie, but why do you get to ask me that?

"Ones, relax. I'm looking out for you. You don't fuck around with a guy like Vargas.

We sat for a second longer, and I started to get up, but he put his hand on my arm.

"Ones. It doesn't help to ask a guy like Vargas about Dasha. It's lose-lose. If he did it, you've hooked a hammerhead, and you're fishing from a paddleboat. He will take you apart and swallow the pieces. And if he didn't do it, he's pissed that you're asking.'

"Freddie. I'm not on some kind of crusade here. The cops think I'm good for it. I'm just trying to find out what happened to Dasha. "

I pushed myself the rest of the way up and was at the door before he spoke again.

"Don't forget the offer on the lawyer."

Chapter Eight

Tully was climbing. He sat down and stood up again three times in the minute that I was watching through the narrow window in the door. Tully understood the disorder, knew the symptoms and tried to master them, tried to control the pacing and the talking, the strobing notions, but it was like trying to repack an exploded Roman candle, repair and replace every torn, burnt shred. He knew what every nine-year-old kid knew—that you can't fix a firecracker…you have to start over from scratch, all new materials. One second, you held a magic wand, and the next, it was burnt and spent, emptier than the space it had been standing in. But he didn't stop trying.

He would sit, and if you caught him in the first few seconds, you might think he was relaxed, composed, one leg tossed over the other, his hands resting on the arms of the chair. But it was like watching an explosion in slow motion, starting with the fingers, twitching and tapping, the foot beginning to rock and kick, the head would nod and twist until every part of him appeared to move and expand but not in concert, the chair no longer a human construct of rest and repose but a living, containing, constraining thing, holding, shackling, grasping and when he came out it was charged, convulsive fulminant, as if against his will. Or something. Then, he would pace in long, anguished strides. The steps you take away from a deed you regret before it's done. He would do several lengths of the room without looking up from the floor, talking but trying to still himself with his own hand to his mouth until he would raise his head and see the chair and begin to wind down, begin to be able to control the pace at which he walked until he could slow enough to slide back into the chair. And the process would repeat itself again. And again. He could do this one, two, five hundred times in succession.

I pushed the door open, and he saw me and was to the door before it had closed, wrapping me in his arms and hugging me hard.

"E. Jesus, it's good to see you. Didn't know you were coming in today. Did you say you were coming by? I usually remember when you tell me you're coming by, but I don't remember you saying anything about today.

He turned and looked over his shoulder.

"Jimi, would you turn the TV down, for fuck's sake. I can't hear myself think in here."

He turned back to me.

"C'mon in, E. C'mon in. It's a good day. I'm feeling good."

He did a Groucho, pretending to smoke a cigar.

"If you know what I mean."

He took a short breath.

"But no. I'm kidding about that. It's under control. I mean, I'm going a little 'wicker man,' but I've got the lid on it. It's all about focus and concentration. Eye on the prize. Control yourself, and you control the world. Or some shit. Did I tell you—me and Jorge are working on an app. He says he can code."

Tully rolled his eyes and made a face.

"You can't trust these fucking guys in here, but you never know—it might be true. It's going to be a gas app. It will give you the price for gas at every gas station within a fifty-mile radius…but not just that. It will calculate how much you would spend on gas to get to each station—you would have to put in the make, model, and year of your vehicle so we can estimate gas mileage—and tells you what station would save you the most money. But I'm not done yet. Get this—we figure out the driving time to each gas station, and we turn the savings into how you value your time. So, if you would save a dollar driving an extra half hour, you would be getting paid two dollars an hour for the extra time and effort. What do you think?"

"You don't even drive, Tully."

"What does that matter? I'm pretty sure Steve Jobs didn't like apples."

I looked at him, and he laughed, short and hard.

"What? A guy can't use the occasional non-sequitur? Or everybody thinks you're..."

He made the circling motion with his finger at his temple.

"You know...a little loopy? Whack-a-doodle. But listen to me—going on here. How're you doing E? Any more news on Dasha? You got that sorted out? I've been trying to figure it out in here, but that doesn't work. I need to be out there..."

He gestured with his head towards the window side of the room.

"To get anything done. I need to be able to ask some questions. Watch their faces. Read the body language. You can't deduce these things. There must be observation. Induction, my ignorant friend. This is no time to be simply thoughtful—this demands action, large, violent men making threats and cracking heads. So, what have you got for me?"

"Well, Tully..."

"Wait, wait, wait. Let's sit down, E. I want to give this my full and focused attention."

The thing was...I wanted to tell him. Tully was always a smart guy. On his slowest day, he was twice as quick as me, but when he was cresting the wave, it was like we belonged to different species.

"The cops pulled me in."

Tully nodded and made a beckoning motion to keep talking. It always amazed me how he could pull all the stray wires back into place for short periods when he had to.

"The word on the street is that I hired somebody to do it."

"They say who?"

"Who I hired?"

"Who's talking."

I shook my head.

"Anything else?"

I told him about Vargas.

"What was your feel? Do you think it was him?"

"I don't know."

"Gut."

I shrugged.

"He didn't feel right for it. Nothing seemed to touch him. It didn't feel like he was holding back because he had something to hide—it was more like he didn't give a shit. Like he was thinking, 'why would I answer this guy's questions?'"

"Hard to argue. I doubt it's Vargas."

"Why?"

Tully jerked up from the chair and started pacing, talking over his shoulder when he wasn't facing me.

"Why would Vargas target you? Before yesterday, he didn't even know your name. He's probably already forgot it."

"Target me?"

"Did you hire somebody to kill Dasha?"

I stared at his back and was still staring when he spun and strode back across the room. He noticed the look on my face and grimaced.

"Relax, E. It's a rhetorical question. Of course, you didn't hire somebody to kill Dasha. But somebody's spreading the word that you did. Would that be Vargas? The cops picked you up before you spoke to Vargas. That means he would already have been trying to set you up even before you spoke to him. Does that sound likely?"

I didn't have time to respond.

"No. It's not frigging likely. So, it's not Vargas. It's whoever spread the story about you. That's the guy you have to find. And if he knows you, you probably know him."

"It's a guy?"

"Or her."

"How do I find them?"

Tully was walking away from me now, peering back at me as he answered. The orderly, Jimi, a guy I hadn't met before, wasn't even trying to pretend he wasn't watching. He was on his feet, standing by the couch with his arms folded across his chest.

"Geez, E. I can't do all the work here. I don't know. Who were the guys who told you? The cops, right? So, either they made it up, or they heard it from somebody. Any reason they would make it up?"

He didn't wait for me.

"Maybe. Puts a little more pressure on you if you did set this up. It could be bullshit –something to make you jumpy. Hope you do something stupid like contacting the guy you..."

Tully looked over at me.

"Didn't hire. There. Happy? So, it's not out of the question that they're bullshitting you. But if they're not bullshitting, you have to find your way back to whoever started the story. That'll be your guy."

"They're not going to tell me who's talking to them."

Tully had walked back the length of the room towards me, and he tapped me lightly on the forehead with the palm of his hand as he spun to walk away again.

"Duh, Sherlock. No, they're not going to tell you. You're the fish. You don't describe the bait to the fish. You're going to have to figure this out. Find the line that leads back to the guy. Find the..."

He smacked his hand hard against his forehead.

" I've got it, E."

He started to laugh.

"This is so sweet. And simple. The beauty of most great ideas is that there simple, E. The wheel. Symbols to represent spoken words. The Swiffer."

"The automobile. The desktop computer."

"OK, I get it. Some great ideas are complicated. But this one is simple. You have a message sent to the cops running the investigation. The message says you have more information about who you—Flint—hired to kill Dasha. And you set up a time and place to meet. The cops will assume the message is from whoever spoke to them before. When nobody shows up for the meet, the cops will be pissed and go looking for the guy who spoke to them the first time. You follow them to the guy. Voila."

I stood up so that when Tully spun around and walked back, I was in front of him. He stopped. I looked into his face without speaking, and he held himself still while I did. Some guys get confused in the manic phase, but Tully was always smart—when he was peaking, his eyes held a hard, frantic intelligence. But they cleared, and that kid, scared and sad, swam to the surface.

"This was a big help, Tully. I wasn't thinking straight about the cops. Not sure I would have been able to figure out how to come at this one."

Tully nodded.

"I've got to bounce, Tools."

He nodded again. I looked around the room.

"You're too good for this."

His head dipped, then came back up.

"Jesus, I want out, E. Not sure how many times I can do this in here."

"Hang on, Tools. It can't last forever."

He started to speak but couldn't and nodded. I put my arms around him. His body shook against me—not crying, the jumpy tension of clenched muscle and tendon. I let him go and left. When I looked back through the window, he was sitting still in the orange plastic chair, hands clenching the arms, but as I watched, the fingers began to twitch.

Chapter Nine

I sat on a bench in the park kitty-corner to the diner, Jimmy's. Not the hip Jimmy's with eighteen-dollar eggs and cappuccino, the Jimmy's that was a corner store with a counter and a few stools. I showed up forty minutes before the sitdown was supposed to happen—not sure why. It didn't seem like the kind of thing that the cops would be scouting.

Evans and Dwight showed up together, pulling in beside the diner in a black Crown Vic five minutes late and blocking the alley, not even trying to pretend they weren't cops. Dwight led the way, both men stopping for a quick look around before going in. Once they were in the diner, I got in the rental and parked so I could watch the diner entrance in the rearview. I didn't figure they would wait long, but it was almost half an hour before they came back out, Dwight still chewing on something. They stood beside the car, eyeing the street. Dwight mouthed something that looked like "motherless fuck " and Evans shrugged, impatient, like "What did you expect" before Dwight slammed the roof hard and ducked out of view dropping into the driver's seat. Evans stood looking at where Dwight had been standing, shook his head, and opened the passenger door. The car was already backing out as Evans slid into his seat and closed the door.

They took the Williamsburg into Manhattan. I had figured whoever was setting me up had been a Brooklyn type, but it looked like I was wrong. They must have wondered about meeting in Brooklyn. The traffic wasn't bad, and I was able to stay with them as they snaked their way across to midtown, Hell's Kitchen. They cruised for about ten minutes, spotted a guy on Forty-Firstpushing four shopping carts, leaning hard to keep them moving, pulled into the curb, and waved him over. The guy was small and dirty, wearing a watch cap and scarf over a long coat even though it was in the high eighties. He looked up and down the street when they waved. I couldn't tell what he was thinking, looking for an escape route, hoping they were waving to somebody else? He took a long look at his carts piled high with bottles, cans, and cardboard and shuffled over to the car.

They spoke for about twenty seconds. I had pulled into the curb on the opposite side of the street, about one hundred yards from where they were talking. I couldn't see what Dwight was doing in the car, but I could see the guy responding. He shook his head twice, shrugging but finally pointing, north and west, over towards the river. They passed him something through the window, not money, maybe a couple of smokes, and pulled out into traffic.

Traffic was picking up, and it was a little harder to stay with them, but they didn't go far, ten blocks north on Ninth to Fifty-Second and a few blocks over to DeWitt almost at the Hudson. They swung onto Twelfth and put their car up on the curb in a no-parking zone. I drifted by and took a quick glance right—they were already out and heading for the thin fringe of trees around the park. I sped up took a right onto Fifty-Fourth, swung, and parked the rental in the bike lane. They had been out of sight for a couple of minutes and couldn't have gone far.

I went in the northwest corner entrance and followed the path around to the B-ball courts, working my way around the dog walkers. There were ten or a dozen guys playing basketball, a mix of black and white, and a handful of spectators. I spotted Dwight and Evans on the far side of the courts, heading towards three guys hunkered around a bottle under a tree. They started to stand up, figuring that somebody had called in a complaint and they were being moved along but Dwight pointed at one of them when he and Evans were several steps away—thin guy in a soiled Hawaiian shirt and grey khaki shorts, dirty white-blonde hair standing at odd angles, looking fifty or fifty-five probably more like thirty-five, a cigarette in the corner of his mouth pointing upwards almost at the sky, smoke drifting in a wan forgotten spiral—and he grinned at first, not unhappy to see them until they each grabbed him by an upper arm and dragged him away from his pals.

I stopped on the edge of the thin line of trees, watching. There were a lot of people about, and I didn't think Evans and Dwight would notice me, but I didn't want to risk getting closer than I was. I wasn't close enough to hear, but the body language was clear—them leaning in, nose-to-nose, the guy looking around for help, arms in the air, eyes wide and startled, shaking his head, pointing around—What? I was here. I didn't send a message.

I couldn't hear what he was saying, but I had a pretty good idea of how it would go. Dwight pushed hard, driving his finger into the guy's chest so that he took a step back and rubbed at the spot, still shaking his head, back and forth, back and forth as fast as he could. Dwight moved the guy back a couple more steps, leaning into him, talking low and tight before Evans slowed his partner with a hand on his arm. The two cops took a couple of steps to the side, talking, heads close, almost touching. The guy started to sidle away, but Dwight stopped him with a look. I took a step back into the shadows of the trees as Evans and Dwight finished talking, swiveling to scan the park.

Something wasn't right. They were feeling it. Evans stepped away from his partner and put his hand on the guy's shoulder, smiling as he did, nodding. Again, I couldn't hear it, but I knew how it would go. You did good. Sorry. Our mistake. Let us know if you hear anything.

They waved him off and took a last scan of the park, then walked back the way they had come.

I thought the guy might fade, look for another spot, but he didn't, his two pals materializing from the trees after the cops were gone. Probably figuring lightning never strikes twice. Too bad for him.

People can't help it. When somebody comes at us with a big smile and their hand out, we smile back, stand up to greet them. He was grinning like a kid who should wear a helmet to bed and his hand was in mine before he realized he didn't know me. He looked even older up close—beat up, a dent over his right eye where something had given and not been pushed back out, lines like shattered glass around his eyes, a trio of deep furrows running from beneath his right eye to a spot above the curl of his mouth, his neck loose and creped, the hint of beach boy gone when you closed in. He could see past the sliver-thin grin now and tried to pull his hand away, but I didn't let him.

"What the fu…"

"Hey, pal. Einstein Flint. Nice to finally meet you."

It took a second, maybe a little less and the challenge fell out of his face, he didn't even try to cover.

"Aw shit, man. You weren't supposed t…Aww fuck."

He looked down at the ground at his feet.

"You going to run if I let go of your hand?"

He shook his head.

"Can't run. Fucking emphysema."

I hadn't noticed the labored breathing from a distance but up close even after saying a few words I could hear the rasp and strain. I released his hand, and he let it drop to his side. He tilted his head at the ground.

"Mind if I sit?"

I nodded, and he settled onto his haunches, then onto his butt. I stayed standing.

"Why are you telling them I hired a hitter?"

He picked at some loose gravel in the grass.

"Why you think, man?"

"I don't know. You got a beef with me?"

He looked up at me, tired but smiling like I was a simple child.

"Beef? I don't even know you, man. Beef. Fuck."

"Then why?"

"Why else? Guy offers me a Kermit to say that some guy named Einstein Flint was around asking about who could he get to put somebody down and how much would it cost."

"Who?"

"Who what?"

"Who gave you the money?"

"Didn't know the guy. Didn't wanna' know."

"Black, white, Hispanic?"

"Looked Mex."

"How old?"

"Fuck should I know? What am I—some kind of "guess your weight for a buck" motherfucker?"

"What's your name?"

He looked up at me again.

"What?"

"Your name. What's your name?"

"Jesse. But round here they call me Hooch."

"Well, Hooch. You've jammed me up good. A friend of mine is dead and the cops think I killed her. And they think I killed her because you told them I killed her. So, you better start thinking harder or I'm going to drag you a little deeper into these trees and beat you skintight. You understand what I'm saying?"

He didn't do anything and I nudged him with my shoe, hard. Under the first rib.

"Ahhhh. Fuck. Take it easy. Gimme a second! I don't know. Thirty? Forty? Not young. Not old. But closer to young than old."

"How was he dressed?"

"Shit, I don't remember. "

"Hat?"

"Yeah. Some kind of ball cap but not from a baseball team. NYC cap. Firefighters? Five-oh? But he wasn't NY fire. Just wearing the hat. You could tell. "

"How?"

He shrugged.

"Fuck knows? You can tell."

"Jeans, slacks, shorts?"

"Shit man—I don't know. Who pays attention to that shit? Not shorts. I would have noticed shorts. Slacks, I think. But boots, for sure. Shitkickers. I remember because they were sharp at the toe and capped—looked like they could gut a fish."

"Anything else?"

"The guy could go."

"He was a fighter? Like a boxer?"

"Nah. Not like that. Nothing where you're wearing gloves—his hands were beat up, couple of the knuckles not quite right."

He looked at my hands but didn't say anything. I knew what he was seeing, the pale nicks against the dirt-brown skin, one knuckle on the right hand twice as large as the others—I had been going for the middle of his face, and the guy had ducked forward, taking the shot off his forehead. It had broken the knuckle, but I had to hit him twice more before he went down, and the second one had busted the joint like a stomped walnut shell. It healed. Just not in the shape of a knuckle. I couldn't think of anything to ask him.

"What now?"

I looked across the basketball courts to the walking path. A young woman in black biking shorts and a red lycra shirt tugged hard on a leash holding a barking French bulldog, preventing it from going after a cowering Golden lab five times its size.

"Nothing. If I need you, I'll find you. For right now, keep your mouth shut. Pretend we never talked. If you see the guy or he gets back in touch with you, you call me."

"So, keep telling people you were looking for somebody to whack your friend?"

"No need to look for opportunities, pal. Don't change your story now."

I couldn't bring myself to call him Jesse or Hootch,

"How will I call you?"

He flinched as I reached for his pocket, but I took the near-empty pack of cigarettes out of his shirt and wrote my number on the bottom.

"If you see the guy or he gets back in touch, you call me. I don't care what time it is—phone me. You do that, and I'll find a little something for you. A little payback."

He nodded. I had walked several steps away, heading back to my rental, when he called out, and I turned around.

"Any chance I could get a little taste now?"

I held up a warning finger and turned away again.

Chapter Ten

She had been following me for a couple of days now. Slim as a twelve-year-old boy, black, her hair razored short, a small gap between her two front teeth, and a blaze-white scar under her lip.

I had seen her in the bar. Twice. The first time, she had been watching and turned away when I looked at her. The second time, she had gotten better at it, and I didn't catch her watching me. I saw her the third time at the other end of the subway crowd waiting for the same train. And now, standing at my bedroom window with the lights off, I could see her standing across the street watching my apartment.

She stood outside the pooled light of the one streetlamp on our block, but I could still see her clearly. She worried at her bottom lip with the thumb and forefinger of her left hand, pushing it together, creating a shallow furrow, pulling it away from her bottom teeth. Her right hand clenched and unclenched against her side. She was fraying, had been for a while, and it looked like strands were starting to snap. I was pretty sure I wasn't going to get any sleep knowing she was standing out there, so I put on my jacket and went into the dim hallway and down the stairs. It wasn't cool enough for the jacket, but it had been threatening rain all day, and I thought it might be more convincing that I was going out for the evening if I put on the jacket.

When I stepped out of the building I looked to the left, away from where she was standing but caught movement out of the corner of my eye, her stepping back behind the edge of an apartment when she saw me in the door. I crossed to her side of the street, looking straight ahead, walking as if I had a place to go until I was across from the shadows where she was standing. I made a sharp left turn, took six or seven long strides, and had her by the upper arm before she could move away. The suddenness had frozen her, and she didn't turn to run until I had her. She twisted her body and tried to pull away, but I held her tight—my index finger met my thumb around her bicep.

"I'll scream."

"Yeah. I don't think so. Why are you following me?"

She jerked against my hand, and I felt her skin twist and burn under my fingers. Had to hurt.

"Let me go!"

Up close, I could see that she wasn't quite as young as I thought—early to mid-twenties, not teens.

"You've been following me for the last two or three days. Saw you twice at Boom's, then waiting for the subway, now here. What's the deal?" You part of this? Part of the set-up?"

She jerked hard, pulling me a little off balance and losing her footing so that she would have fallen if I wasn't holding her. I snapped hard, keeping her on her feet—probably felt like her arm was coming out of her socket. And it will pop if you pull hard enough—but we weren't close to that yet.

"C'mon. Let's take it inside. We don't need a crowd for this."

I should have been paying more attention. It's that she was tiny—I had carried heavier saddles with one hand—and she seemed to have calmed down. So, when she drove her foot into my balls, I let go.

It's instinctual; you go with both hands. I'm guessing it's prehistoric. Maybe if you've rehearsed a lot, visualized taking one hard to the chestnuts, imagined the feeling of swallowing a nail bomb, sucking it deep, right down to the place between your navel and your nutsack, and envisioned it going off in stop time, frame by frame, lead, steel, copper, alloys, box, roofing, finishing, spiral shank, flathead, old-style clout, square-set, in a twisted metal mist that started in the middle and expanded like a mushroom cloud until your knees felt like they folded both ways and your heart congealed in your chest, air and blood as thick and still as poured cement…maybe, if you had gone over that a few times in your head, prepared yourself, you could cup yourself with one hand. I went with two.

She was already at the end of the alley when I looked up, I took a step after her before I threw up. I stayed like that, bent over at the waist in a shallow crouch, one hand on each knee—meatball sub with extra chilis—not the blood and bile and lung meat a first-timer might have expected. I wasn't a first-timer.

The alley twisted out onto Frost Street, but she wasn't there. There was a subway station at the end of the street. She would have headed there. When I got to the turnstiles, I could hear the B pulling out, heading for Manhattan. No sense dropping three bucks to look at an empty subway platform. No biggie. She'd be back. Or not. Either way worked.

* * *

"Hey, Ones."

"Hey, Bobby. How's it looking? "

Bobby V was the early man—from eight to eleven, one on the door was enough.

"You okay?"

"Fine. Why?"

"I don't know. You're looking a little green, man."

"I'm good. Any hot spots?"

"Couple of guys at eighteen could be a problem. We'll see."

I hadn't seen them before. They were Hispanic but not the usual boots and belt-buckle crowd—suits, no tie. Not expensive but not cheap either. They were both sitting on the same side of the table, eyeballing everybody that came in the door. I could see the flush around their eyes from across the room.

"What are they drinking? Zafiro?"

"Nah. Cheap stuff. Beer back."

"Vargas' boys?"

"Could be. Haven't seen him in a couple of days."

"Worth talking to them?"

"Look at 'em. What do you think?"

Bobby was right—these were the kind who would only get worse. They were going to get into it tonight—we could hope that we got lucky and it would be at somebody else's place—that they would have a few at Boom's and make a mess at their next stop. No such luck.

* * *

Things popped after one AM. They had been drinking hard since I arrived at eleven and found a couple of girls to sit at their table, but it hadn't lasted long. Those kinds of guys would always mess it up, say the wrong thing as soon as they got the chance.

They drank even harder after that but stopped smiling. People came in the door and looked away, edging wide around their table, or turned around and left. I gave the word to Mikey before one—no more. Cutting guys off either ends trouble or precipitates it—I was pretty sure how this was going to go.

We should have been close by when the two got the word, but me and Bobby got distracted by a couple of ladies yelling on the dance floor, and by the time we got word, things had already started to come

73

apart. The shorter of the two men had DeeDee by the arm, pulled in close, and he was whispering in her ear. The stuff he would do to her if she didn't get them another drink. We usually try to start easy and see if we can talk our way through it. Most times, you can. But not if somebody touches the girls. Everybody needs to know—you don't touch our girls. And it had already been a bad day. I spread the guy's nose across his face. He didn't see it coming.

First law of bouncing—don't call your shot.

I had to give his buddy credit. He smashed the glass off my forehead before I could turn towards him, and it put me down. Not out, but my ears were ringing, and the room spun. Something warm leaked into my left eye. I was up quick. That was my strong point. I was OK with my hands, but my strength was that I didn't know enough to stay down.

Bobby, on the other hand, had dabbled in MMA and could do it all—grapple, punch, kick, choke—but he loved to punch. He was working the second guy like a speed bag. Bobby caught the guy by surprise after he hit me, and now, he had to hold the guy up to keep hitting him. My guy's face was a smear of blood, but I'll give it to him; he tried to get up. I leaned over and hit him high on the cheekbone and felt something give, and he went back done smacking his head on the wood floor. I straightened up and wobbled, caught my balance, put my hand on Bobby's arm.

"Whoa, buddy."

"Fucker needs a lesson."

"He stopped processing anything about three shots ago, Bobby. Let up. Let's get 'em outside."

Bobby one-armed his guy across the floor, bouncing him off a table and the doorjamb, still pumping adrenalin like a heatwave fire hydrant pumps water, the crowd spreading to let us through.

I wasn't feeling quite as good and hauled my guy two-handed across the floor, spitting twice to clear my mouth. He was heavier than he looked. I was tired, and he almost got away from me and slid down the stairs on his own. That would be all I needed—guy hits headfirst, and I end up on the hook for wrongful death or worse. We pushed them out through the street-level door and dropped them against the wall. Bobby reared back to put a foot on his, and I put my hand on his shoulder, pointing at his boots.

"Not with those on, Bobby, you'll fucking pierce a lung."

He held up and took a deep breath.

"You're right, Ones. But this asshole dinged you good."

He nodded at my head. I put my hand up, and my fingers came away red. I could feel the split, ragged, and oozing blood in a steady trickle between my eye and the bridge of my nose, leaking into my mouth and off my chin.

"Fuck. Feels like stitches."

"No doubt."

I held my hand against it.

"I'm going to get a towel. You call the cops."

* * *

"What the hell happened?

"The guy had hands on Dee, Freddie. End of story."

Bobby was doing the talking. My left hand pressed a bar towel to my head, and my other hand rested against a bag of ice. My fist had puffed up to twice its size by the time we were back in the bar—I hadn't noticed it at the time, but now it hurt like hell.

"Did it have to go there? What did Dee say to the guy? You know that girl has a mouth on her."

Couldn't stay out of this one.

"Really, Freddie? So, you can put your hands on the girls if they smart-mouth you? Slap them around if they don't talk nice? Is that the new house policy?"

"Shit, no, Ones. Nobody touches the girls. But. These fucking guys? It had to be these guys?"

"You know these assholes?

He looked up at me, pissed.

"No, I don't know them, Flint, but you just have to look at them to know they're plugged in somewhere. We're going to hear back on this one."

"Maybe not."

"Mark my fucking words, Ones. We'll hear."

He took a big breath and slapped the table.

"But fuck it. You boys did what you had to do. Let's have a drink... then we'll get you to emergency."

"I'm good, boss. I want to get this sewed up, then get some sleep. It's been a tough day."

"I get it, Ones. Bobby?"

"I'll stick around for a drink, boss."

Freddie clapped his hands together.

"Great. OK, hang tight, Bobby. Let me Uber Flint up, and we'll grab one.

* * *

I was three hours at emergency and, by the end, I was wishing I had taken the drink.

Chapter Eleven

I didn't wake up until eleven and checked my phone. Somebody had called late—four AM—from a number I didn't recognize. I was old enough to remember phones that could wake you from a drunk sleep, pull you out from under a quart of JD and shake the stink sweat loose. This time, no message, and it wasn't a number I recognized. And I only got phone calls from numbers I recognized. Maybe he had something.

They had stitched me up and sent me home with a patch that ran almost all the way across my forehead, and my eyes had blackened up while I slept. I couldn't do anything about the eyes, but I splashed water on the bandage and worked it off—it wasn't much better, the stitches stiff and black against my red and swollen forehead. Nothing a ballcap pulled low couldn't hide.

He wasn't where I had seen him last, but I did a slow loop around the park and found him under a tree on the east side, away from the river. He was with a couple of guys, sharing a forty of King Cobra—could have been the same guys from before. Nobody moved when I walked up.

"Hey, pal."

"Hooch."

"Right. Hooch."

"I called you."

"Yeah."

"No answer."

"What did you want?"

He had been hitting it pretty good. He tried to focus on my face, but his eyes kept sliding off.

"Shit man, what happened to you?"

"What've you got?"

"A taste."

"What?"

"I need a little something-something."

"You tell me what you've got for me, and we'll sort out what you get from me."

He smiled and tried to stand up, made it to one leg but gave up and slumped back down, then spoke like nothing had happened.

"I don't think so."

I squatted down beside him and put my mouth almost against his ear.

"Listen up now, Hooch. Or Jesse. Or whatever your fucking name is. You are going to tell me why you called me, and if you don't, I'm going to drag you away into those bushes, and when I'm done, all they're going to find is gristle and cartilage. Remaining something that doesn't need a team of forensic scientists to be identified will be your reward for telling me why you called. Do you understand me?"

He let his head tip forward, his chin falling against his chest, eyes closed, and I thought he had drifted away and reached out to slap his cheek, but he spoke before I could touch him. I could hardly hear him.

"Drag me, asshole."

It wasn't a challenge. Or at least not one with bared teeth –letting me know that if I was up for giving one, he was up for taking it. And I wasn't. The guy would have come apart like wet foolscap, but I had a feeling he was ready to get torn, bunched, and tossed, tired of waiting for things to get better.

I pulled out a twenty and held it low so he could see it.

'You tell me anything I can use…"

He reached for the bill, and I didn't pull it away. But I didn't let go either. We hunched like that, and then I opened my fingers, and he snapped it back, stuffed it down the side of a worn sneaker. We both knew it was still my twenty, but if it made him feel better… I nodded at him to tell me his story.

"Guy came back."

I was pretty sure, but I had to be certain.

"Which guy?"

He looked up, puzzled.

"Which guy? Shit, you listenin' man? Guy who told me to pass the word that you had put the finger on that girl."

I nodded and motioned for him to keep talking.

"Sheeit man. Who's the fuckin mushhead here? Which guy?"

"Don't make me."

He pulled his foot with the twenty in closer to his body and looked over his shoulder. His buddies had moved off, took the bottle with them. There was him, me and a couple passing with two large poodles who kept their eyes on the dogs.

"What did he want?"

"Checking to see if I had passed the word."

"Did you tell him about me?"

He shook his head too quickly. That was the tell—he had been practicing. Didn't matter.

"That it?"

He shook his head.

"Nah. It's better. One of my boys knew him. Not knew him—not like that. But he seen the guy around. Hey man, you got a loosie?"

"Stay focused, Hooch. Where?"

"Sanchez from across the bridge—says the guy works one of those Mex cowboy bars."

"Your guy's name is Sanchez?"

He barked hard, and it took me a second to realize he was laughing.

"I don't know his name, man. Sanchez, chalupa, a fucking Mexican, brother. Washed dishes for a while in Brooklyn."

"What bar?"

I was afraid to hear this.

"Boom's? Boom Boom's? Something like that."

I got up and left him there.

* * *

"What are you talkin' about, man?"

"You been talking to a skidder down around Dewitt, Bobby. Telling him that I set up Dasha—paid a guy to take her out."

"Are you crazy, Ones?"

Mikey looked over, watching us both, and went back to slicing limes. It wasn't very busy yet, and I had cornered Bobby by the bar.

"I talked to the guy, Bobby. Bum named Hooch; he told me it was you."

"He said it was me? Bobby V? He knew my name?"

"Nah. But he described you—right down to working here and wearing a PD hat."

Bobby glanced down at the cap by his hand on the bar.

"Fuck, Ones. Half the door guys in the city got one."

"C'mon, Bobby. Quit fucking around. You did this. I want to know why."

"This is bullshit, Ones. We been friends for a while. You're good on the floor—keep things loose until they need to be tight. And once we go, you don't take a step back. But if you keep up with this shit, we're done."

I stared at him, and he stared back.

"Mikey, you got your phone?"

"Sure, Ones."

He pulled it out, tapped it a couple of times, and tossed it to me. I flipped it up, took a picture of Bobby V, and slid it back down the bar.

"Email that picture to me, Mikey."

"Email, brother? Why don't I send you a smoke signal?"

"What are you doing, Ones?"

"Nothing, Bobby. I want to remember the moment."

But he knew what I was doing. And I thought I saw something in his eyes—worry?, guilt?…but maybe I was looking for it, seeing stuff that wasn't there.

"Fuck you."

He slid off the stool, picked up his hat from the bar, and walked away.

* * *

Why would he rat you out, E? Even if you had done it—let alone when you didn't?"

He lay on the bed, his arm draped over his eyes. I had told him the story and waited. Tully was deep on the far side—everything took a while—if he answered at all.

"I can't figure it."

"People are fucked."

"That's it?"

I could see the lower half of his face, and his mouth moved as if he might speak, but he didn't.

"Tully?"

Nothing.

"Tully?"

"What?"

"People are fucked?"

"You've got a better explanation?"

"No."

"So, either you're missing something, or people are fucked."

We sat without speaking for a few minutes.

"E?"

"Yeah?"

"I think I'm going to sleep now."

"Okay, Pal."

"You going to stay?"

"For a while."

"Okay."

He was still sleeping when I left an hour later.

* * *

I found Hooch in the park on my second try, showed him the picture.

"This the guy?"

He took a look.

"That's him."

"You sure?"

"Yeah. That's him. Not wearing the hat, but that's him."

I wish I could say I was pissed. I was emptied out.

Chapter Twelve

She was there again. Not the same spot—she had moved down the block, out of sight from my window unless I leaned way to the right with my face against the glass. Which I was now in the habit of doing.

I couldn't figure this out. Maybe she was working with Bobby, but I still couldn't figure his angle, and it didn't feel right. She was scared and small when I had grabbed her—nothing savvy, nothing street. Okay, street enough to kick me in the balls, but her aim had been way better than her form. And how hard is it to get the aim right—as long as you start out between the knees, everything pretty much funnels to the kill zone—it's hard to drift out of bounds.

Why watch me? Hoping to see what? A meeting with the hitter? No way she was a cop. And they were the only ones who were buying the hired killer story. Bobby may have been spreading the story, but I couldn't believe he actually bought it. Maybe Bobby V wanted to keep an eye now that he knew he was made, but she had been on me before I had known about Bobby. It didn't make sense. But neither did Bobby ratting me out.

But I could follow her as easily as she could follow me. Except if I was going to do that, I couldn't stand with my cheek pressed up against the window until I saw her leave. I took the stairs to the basement, worked my way through the scraps of past renovations, and out a rusted door that had a handle on the inside. It took me into a narrow alleyway that came out onto Sixty-First, a block over from the entrance to my place. I walked up to Thirty-Seventh and found a spot short of Sixty-Second, edged up to the corner, and took a peek. She was well down the block looking at my apartment. I edged back and leaned against the Fiesta Latina—shuttered up for the night. I figured she would come this way—wouldn't want to risk walking by my window and have me happen to be looking out.

Shit. I had left the lights on. If I had been smart, I would have shut off the lights before I left—give her the impression I was packing it in for the night. But I didn't want to risk doing it now and losing her.

It took a while, must have been almost midnight when she left. I stayed well back in the shadows, and she didn't even look my way when she came by. She looked back a couple of times like she wasn't sure about leaving but always looking up Sixty-Second—not down to where I was standing. She turned right at Broadway, and I ran up Thirty-Seventh—certain she was heading for the trains. Sure enough, she went down the stairs at Sixty-Fourth. I took the stairs at Sixty-Fifth that brought me out at the far end of the tunnel—more than a block away from her. After the first peek to see that she was heading to the City, I stayed away from the platform and out of sight waiting for the shake and rattle.

I let the front car roll well past before I stepped out—I didn't want her looking down the platform at the train and see me—and watched her get on. I entered the car second from last. This was going to be tricky—I had no idea where she was headed, and I couldn't get close enough to see her inside the train. I was going to have to step off the train at every stop to watch for her.

At least it was late on a weekday, so the train wasn't crowded. A middle-aged woman, sharply dressed, black shift with a short white jacket and medium black heels, was the other passenger in my car. She looked way more Uber than subway, but you could never tell. She watched me step off and on the train for three stops and got off and moved three cars up, careful not to look back at me when she did it. At the next stop, a young black guy pushed by as I stepped off. When I stepped back on, he was hanging from a rail even though all the seats were empty, grinning.

"Don't know your stop, buddy?"

"Long story."

"Aren't they all."

A couple of people got off and on over the next half dozen stops but the kid stayed on. At South Ferry, an older guy got off. I stepped off and looked down the platform—she wasn't moving. No surprise there…. I couldn't see how she could afford this end of Manhattan. Didn't look the type. I got back on, and it was me and the black kid again, still grinning at me.

"That is messed up, bra."

"OCD."

"No shit? I heard about that shit. Socks don't match, and your day is fucked up."

"Something like that."

"Got a cousin with Tourette's—the brother can't start a sentence without smacking his lips. Same kinda' shit?"

"Sorta."

By Seventh Avenue, the train was half full, and it was getting trickier to spot her at the end of the platform. I took the risk of moving up half a dozen cars. The kid shouted something at me, but I couldn't make it out.

It gave me a chance to try my act out on a new crowd—the old crowd had been getting a little antsy. I almost got in the car with the lady that had been in my car at the first stop, hadn't expected her to still be on the train. But she was. Figured it might make her nervous if I followed her to her car, so I spun and moved a couple of cars further up the track.

The girl got off at Forty-Second with a bunch of other people. I almost didn't see but caught a glimpse at the last second. I figured she was changing trains—nobody who lived here rode the subway. I followed her until I saw her duck into the A train tunnel and took the long route so that I would come out at the other end. It was a calculated risk—if the train came right away, she might get on and be gone before I could make it to the platform. But I couldn't risk being a few feet away from her on the platform.

It worked out, and the rest of the ride was almost uneventful. I thought I saw her on the platform at Ninety-Seventh, but it turned out to be somebody about the same size with the same color hair. Almost didn't make it back on the train—stuck my foot in the door before it closed, and I stood there with the door closed on my foot. I was pretty sure I could pull it out if I had to, but I stood as if I couldn't, and the doors snapped open.

We were all the way to One-Hundred-and-Ninetieth before she got off, and it was close to one AM. I followed her up into the street. It had begun to rain while we were on the train. She headed south back up Fort Washington, and I kept more than a block behind her on the other side of the street. She looked over her shoulder a couple of times but not over to where I was walking.

But there was no doubt the girl was skittish. She turned left onto One Hundred Ninetieth and around the corner to a nine or ten-story box apartment building. I hung back when she let herself in the door and was in the shadows when she took a last look around. As soon as she was inside, I moved up the sidewalk and crossed the street. Now that I had a better angle, I could see there was another door between the outer door and the elevators. Probably needed a key.

I walked up the short walk to the doors, and I could see across the small lobby to the pair of elevators. One was closing, almost shut. Had to be her. I stopped and watched the numbers click off. The rain had changed to a fine mist and settled on my face like drifting chalk dust. The elevator stopped at the eighth floor. I pushed open the outside door and stepped into the narrow alcove—pulled on the inner door—you never know. It rattled but didn't open. There was a phone along the wall and instructions for contacting tenants but even if I had known her number, I doubted that she was going to buzz me up. And even if I could get in and get up to the eighth floor, how to find her apartment?

I moved back out to the sidewalk and looked up and saw a light go on in a window almost at the top of the building. I counted up—eight floors. Probably her. I walked across the street and squatted under a tree growing at the edge of the sidewalk and watched, hoping she might come to the window, and I could be certain, but she didn't. There were shadows, somebody moving around the apartment, but nothing that gave me a clue about whether it was her.

It was an L-shaped building and I moved from under the tree and several steps down the sidewalk to get an angle so that I could see both arms of the building. There were lights on in three windows along the long arm and in one window along the short arm. I mapped them out in my head—where the elevator would be and the hallways. I had been lucky so far—it was late, and this was a relatively quiet neighborhood—nobody had come by. But it was New York, and somebody would be along soon and wondering why I was hanging around outside the apartment.

I walked back to the entrance and stood looking at the phone. I could phone a number at random and hope that I could convince them to let me in. But a couple of failed attempts and there might be a visit from the cops. A flicker caught my eye, and I saw that the elevator had been called up to the ninth floor. It hung there and started down. I counted as it went from the ninth to the fifth—three seconds between floors.

I moved out to the sidewalk and several steps away from the door—fifteen seconds to get to the bottom, another two to threes seconds the doors to open, maybe five seconds to walk across the lobby to the doors, so twenty-two to twenty-three seconds before somebody was opening the inner door. I had already counted off ten seconds. I stalled to a count of five and started walking quickly, determined, knowing exactly where I was going. I kept my head down as if I was thinking but pulled my keys out, let them jangle in my hand as if I was getting ready to use them, hoping they wouldn't look too closely. I pulled open the outer door, still not looking up, and at the sound of the inner door opening, I looked up startled, a little nervous that somebody was there at this time of night, slowing to let them get the door open. It was an older guy, wearing a jacket over some kind of uniform, security. He held the door open, barely looking at me, and I slipped past, jogged to the elevator, and caught the one he had ridden down in before it was called away.

* * *

I stood looking at the two doors in the hallway—it could be either. I knocked twice on the left-hand door before a hoarse male voice answered from the other side of the door. I had stepped to the side so he couldn't see me through the peephole.

"Who is it?"

Could be her boyfriend but the voice sounded too old. And there was something about her that felt alone. It was eight or ten steps to the corner of the hall, and I moved as quietly as I could around the corner. The hallway needed a new coat of paint, and the thin carpet was worn, but it was well-lit—overheads every ten to fifteen feet and no missing bulbs. I heard the voice call out again, although I couldn't make out what he said. After several seconds, I heard the door open. There was a short pause, and it closed again.

I waited several minutes then came out and stood to the side of the neighboring door and knocked softly. I heard her padding to the door, and even from the side, I could see the shadow fall over the peephole. I expected her to say something, but she didn't, and I listened to the faint footfall as she walked away into the apartment. I knocked again.

She came to the door more slowly this time and the shadow fell across the peephole again then disappeared but there was no sound of her walking away. I imagined her ear to the door. I waited for her to speak, but she didn't. I reached across and knocked again—little more than a grazing of my knuckles, but knowing she was still close and would hear it.

Still no answer, but she hadn't moved away. I had no plan. What was I thinking? That she would open the door, leaving only the chain on, and I would kick the door open and burst in? And do what? I stepped in close to the door, letting my head fall forward and tapping gently against the door. I heard faint movement inside and imagined her starting back from the door at the sound, staring at where it had come from, breath caught in her throat. I spoke quietly.

"Ma'am, it's me—the man you've been watching."

I don't know what I had expected, but it wasn't an answer.

"Einstein?" Spoken into the edge around the door so that the words were clear.

I pulled back and looked at the door, let my head dip forward again, happy to let it rest against the cool wood, realizing how tired I was.

"You know my name?"

She didn't answer.

"Why are you watching me?"

I waited and was about to speak again when she answered.

"I don't know."

"You don't know why you are watching me? You have instructions, but you don't know why?"

"Instructions?"

"Who are you watching me for? Who has asked you to watch me?"

I could hear her on the other side, not just her voice but her breathing, the sound as her hair or clothes or skin brushed against the door.

"How did you find me?"

"I didn't find you—I followed you."

"No, you didn't. Nobody followed me."

"You got on the R train in Queen's, two blocks from my apartment. You rode the first car to Forty-Second Street and switched there to the A train, third car from the front, got off at One-Hundred-Ninetieth, and walked home. You got in about thirty-five minutes ago."

"Anybody could tell me what trains come from Woodside."

"And what cars you were on? And that a large man, more than three hundred pounds, wearing overalls but no shirt got off at One-Hundred-Sixty-Eighth Street? Looked like he needed a bath, but it might have been the overalls."

We stood without speaking, our heads touching opposite sides of the door. I imagined that I could feel the warmth of her body smoking through the wood.

"Yeah, he stank."

I waited.

"What is my name?"

"I don't know."

"Let me see you."

I pulled back from the door and thought I might fall, dizzy, head spun, too tired for sudden motion. I caught myself and took a step sideways into the narrow field of vision of the peephole. I remembered somebody saying that looking through a peephole was the surest way to die if somebody wanted to kill you—they waited for the shadow to fall fit the muzzle into the eyepiece, and pulled the trigger. The guy had said that it was closer to a suicide than a murder, but I wasn't sure he understood the definitions of either. I wondered if the same was true from the other side—that if you stood at a peephole, you might just as well have steadied the barrel against your own forehead.

I heard the bolt scrape back from the slot and the chain jangle as she slid it from the track and pulled the door open. She stood behind the edge of the door, the right-hand side of her body showing as if the door might shield her if she needed protection. I stayed in the doorway. We stood for several seconds.

"May I come in?"

She didn't answer and waved her right arm towards the single big room at the end of the short entranceway. She looked the same—maybe a little more tired, not quite as frightened. There was one room apart from a small bathroom in the corridor leading into the main room. The stove, fridge, and sink were in the far-right corner, with a small kitchen table set up by the fridge and near a window. Her bed, a Murphy double, came out of the wall in the near right corner, and the room was separated by a large gray leather couch that faced a flatscreen mounted on the wall. A matching leather loveseat was to my left as I came into the room and a glass topped coffee table sat between the couch and the TV. The floors were hardwood, not recently done but still looking pretty good.

"Nice place. What do you pay?"

"Jesus, we've both been in NY too long. Thirteen hundred, seventy-five dollars. Sit down."

She waved vaguely at the sofa and chair, and I sat on the arm of the loveseat. She moved to the end of the couch farthest from me and stood with her hands resting on the back.

"So?"

"How do you know Dasha?"

She stepped back from the couch.

"Who said anything about Dasha?"

"Lady, the one thing I'm sure of is that this has something to do with Dasha. Things weren't perfect before she got killed, but since she died?…….my life's come apart like a bullfrog with a cherry bomb up its ass."

"You really don't know my name?"

I was tired. I was sure I could close my eyes and fall asleep sitting in this strange woman's apartment, and she could decide what to do with me on her own time. I ran a hand through my hair and used both to rub my eyes open.

"No, I don't. Is it important? Because you can tell me if it's important."

She shook her head.

"Mya Jamerson."

"Nice. How did you know Dasha?"

"Used to buy a little weed from her. Hated buying from the guys."

She put on a voice.

"Hey, you wanna' party, girl? Lemme get your head up?"

Then dropped it.

"Just wanted a little weed, man. Dasha was straight business. But then we got to know each other a little bit, share a blunt when I'd come over, mess around a little."

She looked up at me and shrugged.

"I ain't butch, but Dasha was a whole different thing. Girl didn't give a shit."

"Sounds like Dasha."

Even dead, it still stung a little.

"So, that's how you know her, but how do you end up following me around?"

"They'll be coming after me next."

"Who? The guys that killed Dasha?"

Mya nodded. I ran my hands through my hair again.

"Ah, shit. This is going to be bad, isn't it? This is going to be fucking bad."

I stood up. She took another step away so she was backed up against the far wall. It had left for a few minutes, the few minutes we had been talking, but it rushed back into her like an inhaled breath, and I could see it fill her up, the fear leaving little room for any decent parts of her, let alone the best parts. And some of it got into me.

"What did you two do!? What did you do!? You and that psycho, blood-sucking Russian flesh-eater...what did you do!?"

I could see her standing in front of me, Dasha, one hand on her hip, the other holding a cigarette in her mouth, like she had seen it done in the movies... Nicole Eggert in *Blown Away* or Faye Dunaway in *Bonnie and Clyde*, or maybe it was *Mommie Dearest* or Network... or all of those movies. Her hair, long and straight and dyed black, always black, and her eyebrows to match, but the hair on her arms was light, almost blonde. Smiling like she knew something nobody else knew. Every bit it of it learned, practiced, perfected in a full-length mirror...but by the time I met her, it was her. It might have started out as somebody else, but by then, it was all Dasha—as real as any masterwork.

The knocking on the door brought me back.

"Are you OK, Miss Jamerson?"

The same voice I had heard through the panels next door. I looked at Mya, tight against the wall like she was hoping to fall through it. I shook my head, put up a hand, spoke softly.

"Sorry, Mya. It's okay. I'm okay. Tell him you're okay. Or whatever. If you think it's not safe, tell him to call the police, and I'll get out. Whatever. Whatever you need to do."

She moved past me to the door, speeding up a little as she crossed the space near me.

"It's okay, Mr. Varrick. I'm alright."

"I heard shouting."

"You did, Mr. Varrick. But it's OK. Nobody's in any danger."

"Can I see you tell me that in person, young lady? I would feel better if I could see you when you told me everything was OK."

"Sure, Mr. Varrick."

She pulled the door open. The man in the doorway was big but old and run to fat. I turned to look at him and nodded, but he stared at me before he turned back to Mya.

"Okay, Miss Jamerson, but if I hear any more yelling or commotion, I'm calling the cops. Not on you. On him."

He gave me another look and turned back to his apartment. Mya closed the door and came back into the room.

"I'm sorry, Mya. It's been a long day. Long week."

I sat down in the loveseat, not on the arm, sinking into the cushions. Mya stood behind the couch but closer than she had been.

"OK. Tell me what happened."

She hesitated for a second but started.

"Dasha said to come to you if something went wrong—if something happened to her. That you would be able to help me out."

"Help you out of what?"

It was like she hadn't heard me.

"But word was that you had hired somebody to kill Dasha. That you were the one. It didn't make sense. Dasha said you were one of the good guys. That there weren't very many but that you were one of them. And now they were saying that you had paid somebody to kill her. So, I didn't know what to do. If you were the one that killed Dasha then you would kill me too. So, I watched you, tried to figure out if you were the one. But I couldn't tell. There was no way to tell..."

I held up my hand.

"I didn't pay to have Dasha killed. Times I wanted to strangle her with my own hands—now, might be one of them—but I didn't do this. But somebody wants folks to have that idea."

"How do I know you aren't lying?"

I threw my arms out.

"Does this look like somebody that's here to kill you? No gun. No knife. Sitting on your couch with your neighbor waiting by the phone."

She nodded and bit at her lip but didn't speak.

"C'mon, Mya. Give me something."

She worried at her lip with her teeth, then her forefinger and thumb.

"But you could be waiting on the money."

The thing about tsunamis is that the stuff that matters happens at five-thousand feet and one thousand miles away. By the time you're staring up at a cresting wave, it's God flicking the last ash on a dragged-out Lucky Strike…I'm not sure he's even watching.

"Money?"

She watched me closely. Nodded.

"What money?"

She let out a long breath slowly between her teeth so that it whistled like boiled water, her eyes never leaving my face.

"You really don't know what money I'm talking about?"

I shook my head and felt the bad feeling starting to grow. She said money like the M was capitalized. I could see tension drain from her body, but it seemed to flow right into mine.

"Wow. You don't know. You really don't know what happened. I was so sure… Shit, I can't believe this. I…"

I had put my hand up right after Wow. But it took her a while to catch on and stop talking. I waited until she did.

"How much money?"

"A little under a million. We could have had more, but we didn't realize how much money weighed. We had to keep a gun on them, so we could only carry about one hundred pounds. We didn't know it was a hundred pounds at the time. We weighed it later."

"Where's the money?"

She walked across the room to her bed, hunched down, reached under, and dragged out a couple of green garbage bags, pushed one to the side, then reached back under and pulled out a third. I think she expected that I would get up to have a look, but I was too tired. I had seen a million dollars before.

"How much exactly?"

"Eight hundred, eighty-one thousand, eight hundred and twenty dollars."

"Funny number."

"Like I said—we took what we could carry."

"You and Dasha?"

Mya nodded.

"Anybody else?"

She shook her head.

This was the story.

* * *

They had simply stepped into the room. No need to hammer their way in—the door wasn't locked. Dasha was certain it wouldn't be locked because it hadn't been locked the two times, she had served drinks for the game. One of Vargas's boys had a seat away from the table, a couple of strides away from the five men playing cards, but he was scrolling through his phone, not watching the door. And when he looked up, he saw two women—one almost six feet tall and the other coming barely to her shoulder—in full-length black burqas and niqabs, leaving a narrow slit for their eyes.

By the time, he realized it wasn't the halftime show Dasha had pulled a shotgun from the folds of her gown and leveled it at the center of his body and Mya pointed a revolver at the table. Mya's hand shook badly, and the men at the table seemed hypnotized by the barrel of the gun as it jumped and spasmed like she was clutching a fistful of lit firecrackers. The shotgun was plumb-bob level and steady and swung easily between Vargas's man and the table. Each of the men had large stacks of chips on the tables beside them—the cash was stacked on a table against the back wall.

Neither woman had spoken for several seconds, as Dasha had suggested—let things sink in, settle, give a little of the adrenalin a chance to drain before they started the script. Mya did all the talking because there were two men at the table who might recognise Dasha's voice. They had rehearsed her lines a hundred times, but she still blanked for a second after Dasha nodded for her to begin. Dasha had read the long pause, not looking away from the table but quietly feeding her the first word "Gentlemen." No waver in her voice, and it had got Mya started, and once she was started, the words had tumbled out like roaches from a smoking building.

"Gentlemen. Keep your hands on the table where we can see them. If everybody stays calm, this will be over in under a minute. There's no need for anybody to get hurt; it's only money."

When she was done speaking, she lay the revolver at Dasha's feet and pulled four green garbage bags from the second pocket they had sewed into the burqa. She moved around the round table that the five men were playing at, straying closer than she should have until she heard Dasha's low warning, "Girl." and stepped out to the side.

The money was piled behind them on a rectangular table in five separate piles of bundled notes, each containing four stacks of bills about a foot high. Mya opened the first bag so she could swipe stacks of bills into it but didn't get it open enough, and several bundles caught the lip and tumbled onto the carpet. They had agreed to put the money in four bags, but it was faster to fill two bags, and the money would fit, so she did, but when she grabbed them to walk back to the door, she couldn't lift them off the carpet. She looked across the table to Dasha.

Dasha shook her head and raised four fingers. When she did, the guard went for his gun, Dasha caught the movement and pulled the trigger. There was less than ten feet between them, and if she had hit him, it would have taken his head off at the neck.

Mya didn't know if missing was intentional or that Dasha got nervous and missed. The noise filled the room like poured water—louder than she would have believed possible. Nobody heard Dasha pump the shotgun action, but they saw it. The guard left the revolver half-pulled from his waistband and raised his hands over his head, ignoring the blood seeping from the side of his head where a pellet must have grooved him. Vargas hadn't been frozen as long as the other four players and was partway out of his chair when he saw the arm motion and the muzzle swing back onto the table, and he settled into his seat. Mya didn't know if Dasha spoke to her because her ears were ringing, but she saw Dasha nod at her, and it got her moving again—transferring half the money from each of the bags into the other two green garbage bags and carrying them to the door in two trips. They were still heavy but manageable.

When Mya got to the door with the second pair of bags, she looked at Dasha for instructions, Dasha gave a quick glance to the revolver Mya put down a bag and scooped the gun into one of the burqa's makeshift pockets. She grabbed the bag again and was out the door. Dasha had been behind her, holding the shotgun on the table, and grabbed the second pair of bags in one hand before she backed away. But they had been too heavy, and one had slipped free as they were going down the stairs, and Dasha had left it.

They had parked behind the hotel, illegally but in a spot that wouldn't be seen. Now they pushed the bags through the open back windows, Mya got behind the wheel and Dasha into the back seat—rolling up the windows and crouching down so that it would be one woman rather than a pair in the car. Mya had taken off her niqab at the bottom of the stairs and was another young NY woman in a late model Civic.

Two days later, Dasha was dead.

* * *

"How did they know?"

That was Mya, not me. I knew how they knew. I wished I didn't.

"Could be anything."

She didn't speak for a few seconds.

"Her voice?"

What can you do?

"Probably. Vargas…or the other guy. Who was the other guy?"

"Freddie."

"Freddie? From Boom's?"

She nodded.

"Ah fuck."

Chapter Thirteen

Tully looked good—clear-eyed and rested.

"You taking your meds, Tools?"

"Why you ask?"

"You look good."

"And that's only going to happen through the miracle of modern pharmaceuticals?"

I shrugged.

"Yeah. I started taking them. Doc's found something new—doesn't make me feel like I'm thinking underwater."

"Sounds good."

Tully nodded, but I could tell he wasn't that pleased about taking the medication.

"Any news on Dasha?"

I told him everything that had happened. He listened the whole time—no interruptions, no questions. That was a great thing about Tully—he knew how to hear a story. He didn't speak until I was done.

"What are you going to do?"

Telling the story had put me back in the same place—I could feel the vein flickering at my temple like a faulty incandescent bulb, and there was a tight band across my lower back.

"That fucking Freddie—acting like he gave a shit, pretending to help out. I want that fucker. Take him off at the fucking waist."

I stood up and walked towards the windows, then spun, came back to my chair, but didn't sit down.

"He sat there, Sat in that fucking swiveling chair, like a fucking toad on a lily pad, and passed credit card slips across to me. And he knew full well he was the…"

The words caught in my throat. I was embarrassed by the hitch and turned back to the window.

"How do you know it was Freddie?"

"How do I know!? How do I fucking know!? It was Bobby V that spread the word on me, Freddie's boy."

"Any chance Bobby's hooked in with Vargas?"

"Vargas and Bobby V? Where does that come from?"

"Vargas…cartel cowboy, no? I met Bobby, didn't I? Darkish-complected guy? Hispanic of some kind? Guatemalan? Costa Rican?"

"Stop fucking around, Tully. I'm not in the mood."

"Any chance Bobby's got two bosses?"

"Possible, I guess."

"You need to figure this out. You can't go in and take Freddie apart until you're sure who's behind this."

"How do I do that?"

"I don't know. Let me think about it."

* * *

There were two of them, both a little shorter than me but maybe thirty pounds heavier—some fat but not much. One was fronting the boyfriend, a kid, used fake ID to get in, while the other stood too close to the girl, touching her with his body while he talked into her ear. She had backed up against the wall and couldn't get any further away from him. The boyfriend tried to get to her but not very hard—the first man stopped him with one hand resting against his chest and a few words. I couldn't hear what he said, but it stopped the kid. I looked over at Bobby, and he nodded—I would take the first guy, the one facing the boyfriend, and he would handle the one on the girl.

"How are you doing, friend? Everything OK here?"

I spoke to the kid. The guy turned his head to look at me but didn't take his hand off the boy's chest.

"There's no problem here, bra. Me and my cousin are just talking. Eh, cousin?"

"Is this your cousin?"

The boy shook his head. As my eyes swung from the kid to the other guy's face, I saw him looking at something over my shoulder and started to turn. His friend's fist took me high on the forehead and almost knocked me down. I came up hard, driving my shoulder into the guy that had hit me and slamming him into the wall before dropping on top of him. I hit the guy three times by the second he was out, but I couldn't stop the third one—prick.

I was pulling my arm back to hit him again when his friend barreled over me. My head bounced off the wall, then the hardwood floor. When my vision cleared, the guy was looking down at his friend, still on the floor. I tried to stand up but got to one knee before I tipped to one side. He turned to me and raised his boot to drive it down into my cheek. I tried to roll away, but I wasn't going to make it. It didn't matter.

Before he could stomp my skull, he was lifted off his feet and thrown against the wall. He hit hard and slid down the wall, still conscious but dazed. Mikey followed him over and slapped him twice, once open-handed and back, his knuckles popping the man's lips like over-ripe grapes. He leaned down and put his finger in the guy's face.

"Don't move."

He came over and put out his hand. I had to concentrate. He pulled me up. The room spun, and I bent over with my hands on my knees, trying to stop myself from puking.

"What happened?"

"Not sure. Where's Bobby?"

"Haven't seen him."

"What do you mean, haven't seen him? He was with me."

"Nah, bra. When I got here, it was you and these ass-wipes."

"Shit."

I guess my first thought could have been to be worried about Bobby V…but it wasn't. I knew what had happened.

"Can you handle these guys, Mikey?"

He snorted.

"Shit, Ones—tossed tougher salads. No offense."

"I softened 'em up."

He shrugged, a little embarrassed.

"Sure."

* * *

I found Bobby in the alley behind the club having a smoke, the cig palmed, so I didn't see the ember until he brought it to his lips and took a long drag.

"This how it's going to be, Bobby?"

"Yep."

"Cuts both ways."

"Yep."

"What going on, Bobby? First, you feed me headfirst to the cops, and now you serve me up to those pieces of shit. What the fuck did I do?"

Bobby was fast. He came off the wall like a ricochet and if I hadn't been turning away, he would have draped me. As it was, he hit me high on the shoulder and spun me around. I knew what was coming and hunched a little lower and felt the left hook graze across the top of my head. I didn't try to stop my momentum, let my body swing in a full circle, and pushed off from the low crouch, driving him into the brick wall. I heard the wind empty from his body and stepped back, thinking we were done, but he came off the wall again and caught me on the cheek, and the alley sparked and spun. I threw a hard right, knowing now that he would be coming in behind his first shot and hoping he would be where I thought he was. It caught him in the throat, and I heard him gag before hard, big bone, elbow? Shoulder? split the skin over my right eye. That put me down, and I rolled to the left, thinking he would be following me to finish me on the ground, but he didn't.

My vision cleared and I saw that he had staggered back against the wall holding his throat trying to pull air. I came off the ground and dug a hard left into his body. He swung off the wall, still trying to catch his breath, and brought his knee up—I turned enough so that it caught me high on the hip, and I felt my leg go numb, barely catching my balance and stumbling into the far wall. He threw a left that missed but stung me with a right to the cut over my eye and caught me with a left hand to the belly. I lost my legs for a moment and went to one knee before he followed, driving a straight right through my hands that caught me on the cheek. I felt something give and went down. I got back to one knee, working hard to stay upright, and Bobby put his foot on my shoulder and pushed me back over so that I fell into the garbage and debris covering the ground.

"Stay down, Flint. You piece of shit."

"Fuck you, Bobby."

It came out thick and muffled—he had messed me up pretty good. He had already turned away, and I caught him hard in the back, driving his face into the brick wall. We slid to the ground with me on top. I wanted to stand up and even got one hand under me, trying to push myself up, but it slid off, and my face dropped against his back and neck. We lay there for several minutes before he groaned.

"Get the fuck off me, Einstein.

I managed to slide off him and get myself sitting, propped against the alley wall. Bobby lay prone for several more seconds, then sat against the other wall so he was facing me. I spoke first.

"What the fuck, Bobby?"

"Shouldn't have done it, Ones."

It clicked into place.

"Done it. Dasha? You think I took Dasha out?"

"Nah. I know you were here. Hired somebody."

I laughed and winced.

"So, you believed that shit. Never thought of that—figured you were following orders. Who told you it was me?"

"Fuck you."

We sat without speaking for a minute or two.

"Wasn't me, Bobby. You're getting worked."

"Fuck you, Flint."

He pushed himself to his feet and stood over me before turning and heading back up to the bar. He didn't punch me in the mouth before he left. It felt like progress.

∗ ∗ ∗

I would have kicked the door open, but I had done something to the knee in the fight. I couldn't remember when—probably when I bounced Bobby off the wall. The best I could do now was turn the knob—I had to use both hands—and nudge it open with my good shoulder. I slipped in and dropped into the chair facing Freddie's desk. He didn't look up for a few seconds but when he did, he gave a classic double-take—.a full-on Ralph Kramden.

"Jesus Christ, Ones, what happened to you?"

"It was you, wasn't it, Freddie?"

"Who bounced who? You look like you went twelve rounds with a jet ski."

That stopped me.

"A jet-ski?"

"Yeah, y'know. They're like snowmobiles, but they run on water?"

"I know what a fucking jet ski is, Freddie. What's that got to do with…? Who fights a …? Never mind."

I looked at the mess on his desk –the same scraps of paper that he went through to find the credit card receipt—just more of them.

"You sicced them on me, didn't you, Freddie? It was you."

"What are you talking about, Ones?"

"The cops, Freddie."

"The cops? What the f…? You think I rang the bell, Ones? Why would I do that?"

"Why *would* you do that, Freddie? It's a fucking conundrum. Help me out here."

"I wouldn't do it. Jesus. I wouldn't do it. Why do you think I did it? Who said it was me? Why would I talk to the cops about anybody, let alone you?"

Freddie stopped. He watched me. It was time to go. I should never have come up here—not now. There were too many ways I could screw this up. On a good day, I didn't have a plan. And today was not a good day—I felt like a bag of dropped ice. Recognizable but barely. It hit me, soaked me like a heavy rain, dragging hard at every edge. Grief. I got up.

"Fuck it, Freddie. I don't know what I'm doing. I'm all fucked up—I shouldn't be here. I'm sorry."

It was hard getting it out. Like hawking up a hedgehog. But I had to get through the door without screwing this up worse. Not that I wasn't sorry. Fuck I was sorry. But not about Freddie. I stopped at the door.

"But it was Bobby V, Freddie. Bobby was the guy who spread the word. I wonder where he got it from?"

I had almost made it.

***

Mya was waiting for me when I got home. When I stepped from the elevator into the dimness of the hallway, I could make out a dark shadow hunched beside the door—I wouldn't have been sure it was a person. As my eyes adjusted to the light, I could make out her form, crouched and small, a top-of-the-line hiking backpack leaning against the wall beside her. I was pretty sure what was in it.

She didn't move until she was sure it was me, then pushed slowly to a standing position. I stopped at the door of the elevator; the door started to close but bounced open again. She started to speak, but I held up a finger and shook my head. I walked to the door without speaking, turned the key, pushed it open and went into the apartment. When I looked back, she was still in the doorway, the backpack leaning against her hip. I went back to the door, grabbed the pack, took her hand, and tugged her into the apartment then shut the door. I waved for her to sit. I didn't have a couch, just the mattress on the floor and a beanbag chair in the corner, and she took the chair. I stayed standing and spoke quietly.

"What are you doing here, Mya?"

"I. I couldn't. Stay."

"You shouldn't be here. I'm the only connection they have to you so far."

"What happened to your face?"

"Did anybody come by while you were in the hallway?"

She shook her head.

"They could be watching my place, Mya. And if they're watching my place, they've seen you come to my apartment—a young woman who's the same build as the second rip artist. How long do you think before they figure out who you are?"

"What happened to your face?"

I slammed my hand against the wall, and she jumped.

"Who fucking cares what happened to my face! This will look like a day at the spa if they figure out who you are, Mya. They will take you apart. From the skin in. One fucking layer at a time. Do you understand this? It won't be enough to kill you—they will need to send a message…do not fuck with us. Dasha got lucky—she got loose, and they had to kill her before they really got started. You're not Dasha."

It was too much. It was like a wind-up doll in reverse—slow, barely perceptible tremors that grew until her whole body shook. She tried to stand up, but she couldn't get her hands planted solidly beneath her and sank back into the chair. I could say I did it so that she would focus, understand how serious this was but really, I was pissed. I took a step toward her and stopped.

"Shit. I'm sorry. It's not like that. It's okay. I was just… Fuck, what do I know? It's going to be okay."

I could hear her now—her breath coming in sharp, staccato gasps, the sound reminding me of when I was a kid and I would stand at the sink and spin the faucet on as hard as I could, then off to hear the water splash against the gray enamel. Over and over again. The rhythm and rush soothed me. Now it sounded wrong like something about to short-circuit. I touched her arm, and it jerked away. I couldn't tell if it was voluntary.

"Mya. Relax. Breathe. A big breath. And hold it."

I heard her try and fail to hold it.

"That's it. Again. You can do it."

The second time, it caught for a moment and the third a little longer, and she brought it under control until she was breathing hard and even, catching her breath. She was able to cry, and I listened as she wept into her hands. I touched her arm again, and this time she didn't pull away.

"It's going to be OK, Mya. We'll make sure. OK? But we've got to be smart about it. Any new woman that's seen with me is going to be suspect. They'll figure that if the second woman was somebody, Dasha knew she was somebody I knew. It's not true, but it's what they will think. Eventually."

She stopped crying but kept her hands over her face before bringing them down into her lap.

"I'm sorry."

I shook my head.

"I went off. I'm a little messed up—not thinking straight."

Second time I had used those words… or something like them in the last few hours.

"What's in the pack?"

"The money. Part of the money."

"How much?"

"Half. I thought it made sense to split it up."

"Why?"

She shrugged.

"Don't keep all your eggs in one basket?"

"They know me. They know where I live. They don't know you. The safest place for *all* the money is with you."

I could see her starting to go again.

"No. It's fine. You're right. This is probably a good move. Split up the money."

We sat without speaking for a few seconds.

"But it's true, right? What they did to Dasha? What they'll do to me?"

I shook my head again.

"I don't know what's going on. I don't have the players sorted out. It's hard to guess where it's headed. But we'll figure it out. We'll sort it out, and we'll fix it."

Sometimes, I say stuff.

Chapter Fourteen

I introduced Mya to Tully. "Tools—Mya. Mya—Tools."

She had slept over—curled up in the bean bag chair. I was a gentleman but not enough of one to give her the mattress. Not that she wanted it anyway—I had two sets of sheets and changed them sparingly.

It hadn't gone well when I had suggested she wait for me in the apartment while I went to see Tully. She had made the argument that if she had been seen, they would likely come for her as soon as I left. I told her that if they had seen her, they would be coming for her whether I was there or not. For some reason, that didn't make her feel better about staying.

I had given her directions and sent her out the back door, with the backpack. She hadn't felt much better about travelling alone, but she had understood that.

"Wow, E. That's impressive…I've never seen a black eye that started at the earlobe—Hi Mya, nice to meet you—so, when they're punching you, what are you doing?"

"One guy."

"One guy? Really? Now I need to know what you were doing. Because it looks like you were on his side."

He put on a voice.

"I kicked my own ass."

Pointed at me.

" Name the movie."

I sighed.

"Jim Carrey. *Liar, Liar.*"

"Ding! Ding! Ding! Give the man the Scooby-Doo doll! Let me guess—I say, 'Let me think about it" and you nod and go visit Freddie."

"It didn't go like that."

"Did you confront Freddie?"

I nodded.

"Sort of."

"Sort of? Sort of? How does that work? Did you tell Freddie that…"?

He stopped and shifted to look at Mya. Then at the backpack. Then at me.

"That what I think it is?"

"Yeah. It can't stay at my place."

Tully nodded then looked at Mya again.

"So, this is the young lady in question? Is this a good idea for you two to be seen together?"

He held up his hand to stop me.

"Let me guess… she shows up somewhere, your work, your apartment—she's afraid, can't sleep. You let her in, put your arm around her, make her feel better…"

He looked at her, then at me, and laughed.

"Not bad, yeah? Which reminds me—I never see the Amazing Kreskin anymore—is he dead? Or is it that that shit doesn't sell anymore? Cause that seemed like a pretty sweet gig—do the talk show circuit, bend a spoon here, figure out the word in a sealed envelope there. How hard could it be?"

He was amped.

"You off the meds or are they not working?"

"Meds. Why do you have to bring up meds in front of this pretty lady,

E? It makes me sound bad—damaged goods, not all there."

He turned to Mya.

"It's true, Mya. I am occasionally medicated but just so I can communicate with the common folk."

He nodded in my direction without looking at me.

"Otherwise, I end up talking about things that are so beyond his comprehension that I'm not sure we could even stay friends—imagine trying to be close personal friends with a carp. What would you talk about? You're into Chekhov and The Mountain Goats and he…"

He gave a pretend-subtle nod at me.

"The carp, I mean… wants to suck detritus from the river bottom."

"I turned you onto The Mountain Goats."

"Do you see what I mean, Mya? He was this close to saying, 'I'm rubber and your glue…'"

"Tully?"

He raised his hand.

"Sorry, E. I get it. We've got a problem to solve. And it just got a little trickier. No offense, Mya."

"Right. So, any ideas?"

I had to give Tully credit—even when he was going full speed on a single rail he could focus when he had to.

"How did the conversation with Freddie go?"

"Not great. I accused him of ratting me out. He denied it. But he was watching me the whole time. Every time he opened his mouth, he was watching to see what I would do. He's in this."

Tully's face clenched, the skin pulling tighter over the bone when he bit down.

"Jesus, Flint. Just once, could you listen to me? I tell you to…"

He stopped, took two deep breaths.

"OK. Doesn't matter. It's done. How did things end?"

"As soon as I got going, I realized it was a bad idea, and I cut it short, apologized, and got out. But it's out there. He knows that I know about Bobby V and he knows that I think he's the one that gave it to Bobby."

"Did he give you anything?"

I shook my head.

"Denied everything. But it was him. Now I have to figure out if Vargas is in."

"Oh, Vargas is in."

"How do you know?"

"He's the only one I'm sure is in, E. Freddie? It's just money. And I'm sure Freddie likes his money, but this is a one-time deal—doesn't affect his earning power. But Vargas? He can't let this stand. Two girls come in and rip him off for eight hundred K, and he does nothing about it? In his business? He's finished. He's a little girl. He might as well set himself on fire."

"So?"

Tully shook his head.

"I don't know, E. But the first thing is that you guys can't be seen together. I'm surprised they haven't scooped you up already, E. Figuring that you must know who Dasha was working with. But they're going to think of it and when they do—Mya, you don't want to be anywhere around."

He looked around.

"Damn, it's making me nervous having you guys sitting this close in here—Jesus Christ, don't make that face, Mya...I'm kidding. About in here. Not out there. Out there it's got to be as if you've never met. Right now, the trail back to you is through Einstein—you need to stay off that path."

He ran his hands through his hair. I could see how hard he was working—trying to keep the train on the tracks, throwing sparks on every bend.

"I can't think—I need out of here. It's too hard to connect from here—too much space between the dots."

He stood up and walked to the window, raised his hands as if to pound on the hatched screen, then dropped them to his sides, spun back to where we were, and sat down.

"Tools…"

He stood again and reversed the chair, straddled it, his arms crossed across the back. He waggled his fingers for me to continue. I could see the orderly watching us now from across the room. The new guy.

"Tools…maybe we should go…"

"No!" Too loud. The orderly straightened, readying to stand. Tully put a finger to his own lips.

"Shhh. Shut up. Relax." To himself.

" No. No, E. We need a plan." To me.

He started to stand again, but I put my hand on his arm and gave a small nod across the room without looking over, and he settled back.

"Jesus, I'm running hot; need to cool down. Fuck."

"Tools, we're going to go."

"Ahhh, E. Don't do this…you don't have to go. I'm okay. Just gimme a minute. Things are moving too fast here…we need to get things sorted out now…it can't wait. Can't you feel it, E? You can feel it—I know you can. It's out of the gate already, podna', no time to strap in and tighten up, it's time to rake and ride or get stomped. "

He was right. I could feel it. But I had seen this too often to think he could will his way out of it. He was hanging by a thin thread, and it would snap before long—then he would talk and walk until exhaustion, about things I couldn't follow. None of it would help us.

"Stay strong, buddy. We'll be back."

"Be back. Sure. Be back."

I could see him drifting already, following random synapse flashes like a dog snapping at soap bubbles. I tapped Mya on the arm, and we stood up. Tully caught my hand, and I thought I would have to jerk free, but he held it and looked at me hard.

"But not together. You first. Mya later. Never together."

I nodded.

"Gotcha Tools. I'll be back soon. Stay hard."

He tipped his head but didn't look at me again.

* * *

I left first—figured that if somebody was following me, I could draw them away, and Mya could leave without being seen. But we had agreed I would stop at a coffee shop near her place—watch her walk by, make sure she wasn't being followed. If somebody was following me, I was just a guy stopping for a coffee and a bite to eat. Simple as that. Find a table by a window, watch Mya walk by, stay for a few minutes to see if there was anybody following her. Wait for fifteen minutes, then phone her from the pay phone in the coffee shop to make sure she made the last few blocks okay. Then go home. Easy.

The diner was cool and mid-afternoon, middle of the week, not very busy. It was easy to find a booth by the window. I ordered a coffee and a grilled cheese. I was hungry but wasn't sure I could get my mouth around a bacon cheeseburger. We had agreed that Mya would wait twenty minutes and my train had been standing with the doors open when I got to the tunnel, so she was twenty-five or thirty minutes behind.

It didn't take her that long—she must have got lucky with her train too. I caught sight of her well up the street on the other side from the diner window, the same black jeans and loose black sweater she had been wearing slumped by my door. What else?

Except, when she asked if Dasha had left any clothes at my apartment I had said no. There was a white T-shirt and a peasant skirt in the bottom drawer. Didn't seem to bother her a bit to ask for Dasha's clothes. They wouldn't have fit right anyhow. Now, she looked small and hunched as if the day was raw and bitter rather than September mild and she held her head stiff and rigid—it was taking an act of will, not to keep checking over her shoulder. This city doesn't set everybody free—she looked like it had locked her up and walked away. As she got closer, I could see she was wearing her worry like bad make-up, shadowing the underside of her eyes, narrowing her lips, drawing the color from her cheeks—even if I hadn't known, I might have guessed she had taken a bunch of somebody else's money, and now they were trying to kill her. Or something.

Mya spotted me in the window and stutter-stepped but caught herself and kept walking. She crossed the street so that she would pass the diner and where I was sitting, a few inches away. The diner had a window that ran the length of the low yellow-stone building, and as she got to it, she put out her finger and let it glide along the glass. She kept it there as she walked, a long, clean line, but she didn't turn her head or even cut her eyes my way. I'm not sure what I should have done—maybe, placed my finger against the window but I didn't think of it until she was by me.

The waitress came over, refilled my coffee, and took away the empty plate. She was young and pretty and looked at me for longer than she should have. I smiled at her, but she turned away quickly, and I flushed, touching my face, feeling the swelling and tenderness on my cheek and the bruising around my eyes. I didn't spot anybody who looked like they were following Mya. It was New York, so people went by—they always do. But nobody that looked the type looked like they were focused on something up the street, watching. Most people were on their phones, texting talking, or otherwise preoccupied.

I wasn't as sure about me. A guy had come into the diner not long after I had, young, Hispanic, tall for a Mexican, Six feet, six one, and he had looked vaguely familiar like I might have seen him earlier. I had watched him while I was waiting and he didn't appear to be paying special attention to me, reading the Post, and eating some kind of breakfast plate even though it was well after noon. He didn't even look up when I walked by his table back to the pay phone by the washrooms. There weren't many left in NY, but I had scouted this one out and knew it was working.

It rang eleven times before I hung up. Maybe she had stopped to pick up milk. Or the elevator wasn't working, and she had to climb the stairs. I went back to my table and sat with my hands in my lap for five minutes. I counted every second—one to three hundred. The waitress had left the bill while I was on the phone. I paid up and left a big tip…for scaring her. I let two more minutes pass, and I went back to the phone. After the seventeenth ring, I hung up the receiver. My hand shook badly, and I had a hard time getting it into the cradle. I had a moment where I wanted to bang the receiver off the hard black plastic of the phone box until the pieces splintered, and I picked up the largest shard, walked back out to the eating area and drove it into his eye over and over again until the screaming stopped.

I checked the phone number on the slip of paper I had in my pocket and dialed it again, but I knew I hadn't been mistaken. I stopped counting the rings. She either didn't have voicemail, or she had disabled it. I hung up the phone, but it took a few seconds for me to stop hearing the phantom rings.

I wanted to go to her apartment now, but if it was something innocent and they were following me, I would lead them right to her.

It wasn't something innocent.

The guy was gone, but his plate and coffee cup were still on the table. I strode out the door still walking but by the time I made the sidewalk I was running. Her apartment was about four blocks away, and my knee was seizing up as I got there. The building looked quiet, nobody around the entrance. I slowed to a walk, staying across the street and looking across into the lobby as I strolled by. It was empty. I looked back up the street the way I had come and couldn't see anybody. Christ, I was bad at this—run like a madman for four blocks, then stroll by this building as if I'm out for an afternoon meander through Washington Heights. If anybody was watching, I might as well have tagged her building with both of our initials and the amount of money they had taken. Too late now for the subtle approach.

I crossed the street, stepped into the outer lobby, and ran my hand up and down the buttons—I got several voices talking at once, but somebody must have been expecting visitors…the door buzzed, and I pulled it open. The elevator was sitting on eight but started dropping before I hit the button—I stood back from the door, watching as the light slid from number to number until it stopped. I couldn't slow my heart, and my breath came short and fast—if there was one guy, I was going in hard and low, drive him into the back wall. If there was more than one, I wasn't sure. The doors slid open, and the elevator was empty. I stepped on, took several deep breaths, trying to slow my pulse, clear my mind.

I hit eight, and as the elevator passed the second floor hit seven. What was I thinking? They might be watching the elevator from the hallway right now. And even if they weren't, the sound of the bell would bring them running. When the elevator stopped and the door opened, I stuck my head into the hallway. Empty. The stairwell was at the far end of the hallway to my left. I stepped out and walked down the hall, pushed the door open, catching it behind me so it wouldn't sound, and crept up the stairs. I heard the elevator bell as I got to the stairwell door and pushed the door open enough so that I could peer up the hallway—if anybody was there, they would be watching the elevator. The hall was empty. I waited for somebody to come out of Mya's room, but the hall stayed empty and quiet. I stepped into the hallway and let the door close behind me, sharp and loud. I waited to see if that shook anything loose, but nothing stirred.

If I wasn't looking, I wouldn't have noticed—probably knocked and walked away when she didn't answer. But, of course, I was looking. They had jimmied the door. There were scratches in the paint and a depression where they had wedged something between the door and frame and levered. They had been waiting for her in the apartment. I turned the handle. pushed the door, and it drifted open.

"Mya?"

They had left her tossed in the corner like a wind-snapped umbrella. It had been more than thirty minutes since she had trailed her finger along the diner window, so they had time. They had worked with something hard and blunt—a baseball bat, probably. It had caved in the right side of her head. But that had been the last one. There had been a lot before that. Her leg was caught under her in a way that a body didn't bend, and her right arm trailed across her lap loosely jointed in four places. Her left eye was open and staring down her body as if stunned silent, by what had been done to her. I should have held her, but I didn't know how.

I looked under the bed. The money was gone.

* * *

I don't remember getting on the train. But I remember seeing the guy. I wouldn't have seen him except that I stepped on the train, then backed off to see what train I was getting on. He must have been worried that I was trying to drop him and got off the train too. I saw him down the tracks, looking around as if he was confused and unsure what to do. Same tall Latino who had been in the diner eating breakfast and pretending to read the Post. It brought me back. He was four cars away, and when he caught me looking at him, he let his eyes slide away as if he had been giving me a passing glance. I covered the four car lengths in a couple of dozen long strides.

The first shot took him under the eye and put him down. I don't know what he thought was going to happen, but he didn't even get his hands up. He tried to get up, and I let him get to one knee, and caught him by the front of his jacket with both hands, and ran him three short strides across the platform and into the cement wall. His shoulders hit first, but the back of his head whipsawed against the wall, and his eyes rolled white and wet. I tried to hold him up against the wall so I could hit him again, but he was a dead weight and slid down the wall into a sitting position, then tipped to his right. I pulled him up and punched him three times, losing my grip on the second shot and having to pull him up off the subway platform by his jacket to hit him the third time. He wasn't dying fast enough. I looked around for something heavy, hard, sharp.

She was maybe fifteen and didn't look much like Mya—the same slight build and hunched, frightened shoulders but blonde hair streaked with green and a trail of acne across both cheeks. She stood with her hands over her mouth, watching, unable to move. It was the hard breath spasms that reminded me of Mya like she was inhaling terror and exhaling any confidence that the world was a place where she could sleep without dreams. I let the guy's head fall to the ground and straightened. I held her eyes and started to speak, but there was nothing to say. I walked past her, through the turnstiles, and up into the streets.

* * *

I stood back in the shadows of the alley, watching my apartment. I couldn't remember if I had left the kitchen light on—it was on now. But it didn't matter…they would have been in already—found out the money wasn't there. Now, they would be waiting to scoop me up—take me somewhere and work it out of me. Part of me wanted to walk through the front door and bring them out of the dark, bring them to me as if somehow my rage was enough—enough to burn them to bone and ash and grind them to a thick paste that I could use to paint Freddie's eyes before I tore them from his head. But I knew it couldn't. There would be several of them, and it would end with me lying in my own piss, shit, and blood and them in Tully's room counting the cash while his body cooled. I slipped back down the alley and out into the street one block over.

They must have spotted me watching the apartment because they were waiting for me as I came out of the alley. They would have had me if the first guy had been more patient and waited for his buddy, but he couldn't wait—he grabbed me as I stepped out of the alley, one arm around my neck and the blade against my side. I spun to my right, away from the knife, driving my right elbow into his head. He went down, but I stayed tangled up in his arm and went with him. If his buddy had been there to hold me down, it would have been over, but he was up the block, running, but still two hundred feet away. I scrambled up first, caught the guy hard on the side of the head with my heel, and he slumped back to the sidewalk. And I ran.

I had a forty or fifty yard head start and I stretched it to ninety yards over the first couple of blocks but my face and ribs hurt and my knee was locking up again. I was a block and a half from the subway stop when I heard the train pull into the station through the sidewalk grates. It would be close, but there was a chance. I picked it up and lengthened the gap. I risked a look back and could see that he was still coming hard but flagging. But so was I. I couldn't keep the pace up for much longer.

I grabbed the rail and spun down the stairs, taking them three at a time. I hopped the turnstiles, almost tumbling an older woman coming out of the tunnel. The tunnel heading to the city was empty—it was an eastbound train. I took the second flight of stairs in a couple of long bounds, hitting the bottom and pitching forward, almost falling down, jarring a bolt of pain from my knee to thigh, but catching myself with one hand and stumbling forward. The train was still there, but the doors were already starting to close I lurched forward three steps and thrust my arm through the narrow gap, and it closed around my bicep, and the train started to edge forward. I heard a clatter on the stairs behind me, but I wasn't able to turn with my arm in the door. I could see the engineer looking out the window up the track, shaking her head, and I pointed at my arm.

"Open the fucking door."

She let me jog beside the train for a couple of steps before the doors snapped open. I had been leaning hard on the door, and when it came open, I fell into the car, landing hard on the floor. A couple of people looked down at me —the rest looked at their phones or books or laps. New York City. Falling saved me. By the time I stood up the doors were closed. The guy was standing on the platform, peering into the cars and around the platform, trying to figure out where I had gone. When I stood up, he saw me and made a move for the door, but the train was already rolling, and I stood up tight against the window, staring back at him as the train picked up speed and he got smaller on the platform and disappeared as we dipped into the tunnel.

I rode the E train four stops east to Woodhaven, dozing for a few seconds between stops, coming awake as the train slowed at each platform. At Woodhaven, I hopped off and headed back the way I had come, ducking down as the train rolled through the Sixty-Fifth Street stop, but there were only a few people on the platform and none I recognized.

I had no idea where to go. Two weeks ago, I could have gone to Dasha or Freddie or Bobby, but now there was only Tully. I would go to him, but not tonight—he was going to be riding a rough bronc for the next twenty-four to forty-eight hours and wouldn't be able to help me. I changed to the B train at Seventh Avenue in the city and rode it to One-Hundred-and-Tenth, not sure where I was going but wanting to be far away from my apartment. It was almost midnight, and I wandered west to Amsterdam on One-Hundred-and-Tenth and walked a couple of blocks north to stand in front of the church, looming huge and foreboding over West Harlem. The night had cooled, and I wished I had grabbed a jacket from my apartment when I left.

I walked a half block back the way I had come and slipped into the park beside the church. The first bench was taken, a curled shadow. I couldn't tell if it was a man or woman, but the second bench was empty, and I sat down. I dozed sitting up for half an hour, then curled on my side and slept until just before dawn.

I woke cold and shivering, and it took me several seconds to piece the story back together. Dasha dead, Mya dead, Cops wanted me in jail, Freddie and friends wanted me dead, four hundred thousand dollars stashed under my best friend's bed in the nuthouse—didn't seem like a story that had a happy ending. I couldn't figure out how to back out of this one. But I kept thinking about the cop, Evans, the one who looked like we were sharing a joke even though I had no clue what the punch line was. Maybe he would listen. And I couldn't figure out what else to do.

* * *

I dozed in the hard, plastic chair. I had cooled my heels for fifteen minutes in the outer hallway while the duty officer had tracked down Evans and Dwight, and then he had left me here in the interview room for another thirty minutes. I didn't mind. It was warm. My head came up when I heard the outer handle rattle. They both looked pretty fresh, like their day was just getting started—I was pretty sure I didn't. Evans didn't say anything, but Dwight couldn't resist.

"Sheeeit, Flint. You look baaaaaad. And I don't mean Shaft bad, I mean like shit. Is that how you get rid of assholes at Boom Boom's…they punch you in the face until they get so fucking arm-weary they have to go home? You're supposed to do the bouncing, man, not get Dunloped all over the fucking neighborhood. Did you think to maybe block one or two…or duck maybe? Damn Flint, just because they throw 'em doesn't mean you have to c…"

Evans held up his hand, and Dwight trailed off.

"You wanted to see us?"

I nodded.

"What about?"

"There've been a few developments."

Like what?"

Evans pulled up a chair across the table from me, but Dwight stayed on his feet, shuffling closer to the wall so he could lean against it. He dug around in his pocket, pulled out a toothpick, wiped it on his shirt cuff, and stuck it in the corner of his mouth. He looked over and noticed me watching and flushed.

"Fucking cigarettes. Gonna' quit if it kills me. Ever had a sliver in your tongue? It's like getting a sunburned dick… shouldn't happen."

"Like what, Einstein?"

I looked away from Dwight and back to Evans.

"You still think I'm good for Dasha?"

"Fuckin-A!"

That was Dwight. Evans grinned.

"Dwight likes you for it. And he usually has pretty good instincts. But I gotta' say—I'm not convinced. Maybe, if you hadn't been working, if we could pin it on you—you actually putting the bullet in her head. But you don't seem like a guy who would get somebody else to do your dirty work. "

"Glad I've made such a good impression, Detective."

He grinned again.

"Yeah. So, what have you got?"

"I found the guy who ID'ed me as putting the hit on Dasha—burnout named Hooch who hangs over at DeWitt."

Dwight stood up from the wall, but Evans kept his face blank and eyes on me. I kept going.

"He was fed the story by one of Freddie Riley's boys—a guy I work with at Boom Boom's. Bobby V."

"Why would Freddie want to jam you up, Einstein?"

I looked at him for a long time.

"He's a player, Detective. Big stakes. Private game."

"We've heard talk about some big games."

"Well, this game got jacked, ripped and rolled."

That raised Evans' eyebrows. Dwight came off the wall again.

"This is bullshit, Rich!"

"Dasha?"

I hesitated.

"How much?"

"The number I hear is almost a million."

"She do it alone?"

I had been expecting this one.

"Don't know. The details aren't on the street."

"Be tough to do on your own. Carry the money and keep them covered. Sounds like a superhero."

I shrugged.

"So, Freddie gets chumped for a million dollars. Figures out it's Dasha, kills her, and tries to pin it on you? Is that your story?"

"That's about it."

"How is that better than 'She dumped you, you got pissed and killed her'?"

"I get it. But that's not the story you have. You have an angry boyfriend who sets up a hit. Angry boyfriends don't set up hits—they kill in a rage. And talk to your boy, Hooch…if you haven't already. He'll describe the guy who fed him the story. Check it out."

Evans phone must have vibrated because he pulled it from his pocket, looked at the number, then held up a finger to me and took the call. The person on the other end did almost all the talking. Evans grunted a couple of times—

"Where?"

He nodded twice.

"How?"

He nodded again, and I saw his eyes flick to my knuckles, swollen and scraped, and away before he hit the disconnect button.

"Can you hold a minute, Einstein? We have to take this? But I have a couple more questions. "

"I can stay. But can I use the washroom?"

Evans was still looking at his phone as if waiting for answers to show up on the screen.

"Sure. Down the hall, second door on the left."

I could feel his eyes on me as I walked down the hall, and when I turned left and pushed the door open, he was still standing, watching. I stepped into the bathroom and stood by the door for a count of fifteen, then stepped out as if I had forgotten something. The hallway was empty. I turned left down the hallway, another left to the lobby, then across the floor and out the door into the sunlight. I wasn't sure what Plan B was.

Chapter Fifteen

I watched the hospital from a small coffee shop down the street. If they had found Mya there was a chance they had eyes on it, too, so the front door wasn't an option. But there had to be other entrances.

* * *

A couple of the kitchen staff sat smoking outside the back entrance to the hospital cafeteria—a skinny white guy with long blonde dreads and a tall Asian guy with a tattoo curling up from under his whites almost to his chin. It had been two different guys an hour ago, and I had hoped that when they went back in, they would leave the door open, but they didn't. Someone had placed a plastic milk carton against the door frame, but they had kicked it to the side when they went back in so that the door closed and locked behind them.

Now, it was these two. I could borrow a uniform and a trolley and pretend I was making a delivery…but who had time for that shit. I threw the knapsack over one shoulder and started walking, brisk but not hurried, didn't even pretend I was going to walk by them, heading straight for the door. Turning a little sideways to get by the Asian guy squatting on a second flipped milk carton, I took the last couple of steps to the door. He shifted a little to make space, and the carton scraped against the rough pavement, but the natty dread guy spoke up.

"Hey man, you sure..."

I didn't slow down or answer; I just caught the edge of the door, flipped it open, and walked through. I was in a narrow hallway lined with empty boxes waiting to be broken down, but I could hear the sounds of the kitchen coming from an open doorway up the hall on my left. I caught my foot on a box and almost went down but righted myself and ducked left into the kitchen.

The dish pit was on my left, and swinging doors leading out to the dining area to my right. There was nobody on dishes, but there were three guys behind the heat lamps, one at the grill, and a couple of guys prepping colds. The guy at the grill looked over his shoulder and stopped when he saw me, but I kept walking out through the swinging doors and into the main sitting room. A couple of people looked up from their food at the sound of the doors swinging open, stared for a couple of seconds, then looked back down. I threaded through the tables and out into the hallway that led to the lobby and the elevators. The kitchen guys might be talking to security, but I doubted it.

They could have somebody watching from the lobby, so I took the stairs. Tully was on the fourth floor. I ran the stairs two at a time for the first couple of flights, but my knee wouldn't stand for it, so I slowed for the last two. I held my breath, opened the door from the stairwell, but no bells went off. The door to Tully's ward was at the end of the hallway. Before stepping in, I peered through the wire-reinforced pane. I hadn't been able to warn him I was coming or that we had to go. He was sitting in one of the orange chairs, staring at the window—I could see his profile, but he looked calm and still. I pushed through the door, and he turned at the sound but didn't stand up, just looked me over. I walked over to the chair, he stood up, and we hugged. He whispered in my ear.

"What the hell you wearing, Huggy Bear?"

I had picked the stuff up from the Housing Works on Thirty-Fifth Street—a tie-dyed hoodie with" Fuck da Po-Po" stenciled on the back, a pair of worn camo pants with button-down pockets down both legs. And a wide-brimmed Navy fedora.

I did a slow twirl, and Tully leaned in again.

"It's time?"

I stepped back and nodded. He looked over to where the orderly was sitting. The new guy.

"Jimi, my buddy and I are going to visit in my room—maybe watch the game…cool?

He nodded.

"No problem, Troy. I might stop by to check the score."

We walked past him into the hall that led to the patient's rooms.—I caught him shaking his head at my get-up. As soon as we were in the hallway and out of Jimi's sight, Tully picked up the pace.

"Let's go, E. We have ten minutes—he'll be by to see how we're doing."

We ducked into his room, and Tully shut the door behind us. I emptied the knapsack onto his bed, and he pulled the green garbage bag out from the bottom of his closet. I had stuffed an identical knapsack into the bottom of the one I had been carrying along with a pair of worn jeans and a plain white T.

"Money first."

We moved it quickly from the garbage bag to the backpacks. There wasn't a lot of leftover space…four hundred K took up a lot of room.

"Maybe we should leave one of the packs here?"

"Bad idea, E. What do you think will happen when they figure out I'm gone—they'll be taking this room apart. They won't miss two hundred K in wrinkled twenties. If you want it, we have to take it now."

I nodded.

"I don't get this, Tools—you signed yourself in…why can't you sign yourself out?"

"Not how it works, E. Once you're in, you're in. If the docs don't want you released, they file an affidavit saying you aren't fit to leave. It would take six months and a team of lawyers to get me out of here."

I stripped off the camo pants and hoodie and put on the jeans and t-shirt. Tully was bigger than me, but the pants and sweatshirt were baggy, so they fit over the khakis and polo shirt he was wearing. He pulled the fedora down low over his forehead and stood at the mirror on the back of his door.

"Shit E, I know you wanted conspicuous, but did you have to pick a frigging Hallowe'en costume?"

I shrugged.

"Not the worst outfit I've seen on you."

"Screw you, cowboy."

"Don't slow down when you go through the door. If he catches on and shouts something, keep walking. As soon as you're through the doors, it's a hard left. The stairs are at the end of the corridor. Nobody will be watching for you, so go left out of the stairs on the main floor, through the lobby, and out the door. Even if Jimi sniffs that something's wrong, he's not going to get things sorted around downstairs soon enough to stop you. Oh yeah…"

I reached into my backpack and pulled out a thin sheaf of twenties.

"Take a cab—no sense messing with the trains. I'll meet you at Bryant Park, three o'clock by the ping pong tables. You might want to ditch the hoodie and hat."

"Why the city?"

"I can't stay at my apartment anymore. They're going to have it nailed down. We'll get a room and figure out what to do next. I've got a few ideas."

Tully looked at the money in his hand.

"Should we be spending this? Might be that we'll need to buy our way out."

"Fuck that. They're not seeing dollar one of this money. I don't care who spends it, but it won't be Freddie…or Vargas."

Tully gave me a long look.

"Listen close, E. What if it's the only way out?"

"What are you asking, Tools?"

"What if the difference between breathing and buried was four hundred K? Are you good?"

I shook my head.

"Won't go that way. They'll want us dead with or without the money. Probably best to spend it so when things get tight, we won't fool ourselves that the money can get us out."

Tully nodded.

"That's my take, too."

He tugged the hat a little lower and grinned.

"Bryant Park? Three PM?"

I nodded, and he was out the door. I counted to two hundred and followed. Jimi was getting up as I went by and didn't look at me twice… but he would realize something was up when he checked the room.

Chapter Sixteen

We sat in the hotel bar pushing the condensation rings around on the bar top with our glasses, both drinking Sprite. The Yankees played the Red Sox on the TV on the wall—they had been up nine-zero, but the Red Sox had scored four runs and still had men on base. They were still in the hunt for a wild card spot, but they couldn't seem to keep a streak going—win one lose one. We had taken a room in a little boutique hotel on the Lower East Side and dumped the money in the closet.

"You're sure she was dead?"

"She was dead, Tools."

"How do you know?"

"Don't do this—she was dead. No doubt."

He nodded.

"I know. I know."

We sat for a couple of seconds.

"But how did you know? Did you check to see if her heart was still beating? Did you check to see if she was breathing? Did you…"

"Christ, Tools. They broke her skull with a baseball bat. There were pieces of her brain on the floor. She was dead."

"I know, E. I know. I thought that maybe…"

He pinched the bridge of his nose.

"Fuck."

He swirled the ice in his glass and raised it to his mouth as if to take a drink but stopped and put it back down on the bar.

" You think the guy in the diner did it?"

I shrugged.

"Probably not the hitter. But he was in it."

"How bad was he?"

I shrugged again.

"Freight trained him, Tools. Might not have let up in time."

"Good. It's good, E."

"Don't worry about me, Tools. I'm OK either way. But it's Freddie and Vargas that have to pay."

"You sure about Vargas?"

I had to admit I wasn't.

"He was at the table."

"There were four guys—we taking them all down?"

I shook my head.

"Nah…other two just played poker."

"How do you know Vargas wasn't just playing poker?"

"Fuck, Tools. I don't. It doesn't smell right. It's like you said, he couldn't let it stand."

"So, what do you want to do?"

"I don't know. I don't know."

"Freddie would know."

* * *

"I don't get it—it's never closed on Sundays. It's our biggest night."

We were standing across the street and a block down from Boom Boom's. I had picked up a cheap grey hoodie at a TJ Maxx on Eighty-Sixth Street and I had the hood up and hanging low across my forehead. Between the hoodie and the dark, I wasn't worried about being spotted.

We watched a young Hispanic couple try the door and peer through the window before walking away.

"You got keys?"

I shook my head.

"No. Freddie had a set and maybe, L'il Mikey. But there's a back door. You never know."

We got to the back door from a dead-end alley that opened out onto the street behind Boom Boom's. This door was never locked except when Boom Boom's was closed down tight and it was locked now. I looked up to the edge of the building four stories up. I could see where the darkness of the wall broke against the lighter grey of the sky.

"It's a flat-top. Sometimes the floor staff will grab a smoke up there when Freddie's not on."

Tully wasn't paying attention

"Did you hear that?"

"What?"

Something from inside. Voices, maybe."

"You sure?"

"No. But it sounded like it."

I reached up to pound on the door, but he stopped me.

"E. If somebody's in there, they locked the doors. They aren't going to answer because you're pounding on the door. And if they do, it won't be with good intentions. Can we get to the roof?"

The guy was always paying attention.

"There's a couple of feet between Boom Boom's and the apartment building next door. Dasha used to sneak in that way when she was late for a shift and hungover—make it look like she had been here all along. When she wasn't hungover, she'd rather have the fight. There's no lock on the door to the roof but we'd have to get buzzed into the building next door."

"How will we get buzzed in?"

"Jesus Tully, how long have you lived in New York?"

We walked up the alley, circled the block around to the building beside Boom Boom's, and pushed open the door into the outer alcove. I waved at the door.

"Get ready."

"Ready for what?"

"Quit fucking around and put your hand on the door."

I found the speaker to the left of the list of names for the tenants and slapped my hand hard across the intercom. Nothing. Tully stepped back.

"What the hell, E?"

I reddened a little.

"Never mind, Tools. Get ready."

I cupped my hand and slapped the intercom again, and the buzzer sounded.

Tully had been standing with his hands on his hips watching me and had to jump forward the catch the door and push it open. We moved into the small lobby.

"Sheeit, E. How did you do that?"

"Yeah. I don't know how it works. Doesn't work all the time but seems to work on most of the older systems. From my bike messenger days. Those guys know all the tricks."

"Probably creates a sound that covers most of the frequency range in the DTMF scheme."

"What?"

"You really want to know?"

"Yeah. No."

We took the stairs two at a time. My one concern was that the lock had been fixed, but it hadn't. Tully jumped up, grabbed the handle, and pulled the stairs down. I had expected the hinges to shriek as they came down, but they were relatively quiet. We didn't wait to see if the noise would attract any attention—clambered up the stairs, out onto the roof, and pulled the stairs up behind us. The night was cool but not cold, and it felt good to be out of the narrow hallway and up on the roof. Tully walked over to the edge closest to Boom Boom's.

"You said a couple of feet."

That's what Dasha said. I've never been up here."

"It's more like six feet."

"How long do you stride when you're out for a run?"

"Sure. But not over a thirty-five-foot drop to broken asphalt."

The lip of the building we were on was about eighteen inches above the scattered gravel surface that covered the roof. I took a ten-step run, planted on the lip, and launched myself. I almost made it across the lip on Boom Boom's side but caught my heel as I landed and tumbled forward gouging deep scrapes across both palms.

"That made me feel better, E. You showing how simple it is. I'm feeling confident now."

"Could you keep it down, Tully?"

He ignored me. His push foot seemed to slip a little when he took off, but he cleared the lip easily and stumbled forward but held his balance.

"Did you slip a little there?"

"Yeah, but it really isn't very far."

"Prick."

"Hey, what can I say—I've got some hops, gimpy."

"Hasn't stopped you from being batshit crazy."

"Mental illness is not a joking matter, my crippled friend. If I didn't know you were petty and envious, I might think you were small-minded and mean-spirited."

"Give me a hand with the door."

A heavy hinged door covered the stairs leading down into Boom Boom's, and we both took a side and flipped it back. A person coming up to the roof from inside would have been able to push it back on their own, but it would have been hard work. The stairs were hooked up parallel to the roof. We unhooked them and lowered them by thick cords curled into the crook of one step. We had stopped talking now—there had been no need to signal. We could already hear the voices coming from the floor below. Too far away to make out the words but the tone was enough.

The stairs dropped us to a spot about ten steps from Frankie's office, and when we reached the bottom, we could tell the sounds weren't coming from there. The voice was coming from the floor below, the bar floor. I couldn't make out the words, but I could hear the threat and tension. I had heard it before. I knew that voice.

I signaled to Tully that I was going down but that he should stay where he was. He shook his head. I crept over to where he stood and put my hand on his arm and leaned into his ear.

"It's okay. I know the guy."

He pulled back and shook his head again and made a gesture—him and me. The guy was a pain. I nodded and started down the stairs. I could feel Tully at my back.

"Hey, Bobby. What's the stitch?"

He had been facing the stairs but not paying attention and didn't look up until I spoke. He had been talking to the man tied to the chair. I have to give him credit—he didn't even jump a little—his eyes didn't even widen. I could see he was still bruised around one eye where I had hit him, and I felt a little bit better about that.

"Nothing, Ones. Just hangin'."

He jerked his chin at Tully over my shoulder.

"Who's your friend?"

"Nobody you know."

I nodded at the body slumped in the chair. I recognized the blood-soaked shirt and beret on the floor beside the chair.

"How's Freddie doing?"

"Not so good."

"Still breathing?"

Bobby leaned forward and put his ear to Freddie's mouth, then straightened.

"So far."

"Guess you worked it out, Bobby."

"Yeah. Started working through the story, and the joints weren't holding. Talked to Mikey, and he straightened me out on a few things. Figured I needed to talk to Freddie. "

"I see that. How's it going?"

"He's a tough old fucker. Wouldn't have guessed."

"How's this going to end?"

"That's up to Freddie."

"He did it, Bobby. You got to hear him say it?"

"Yep." And Bobby hit Freddie.

It was a wet sound, like swinging a soaked towel against a cement pillar. The blood pooling under Freddie's eyes and at his neck rose like bluebottle flies shooed off a dead dog and splashed down and lost onto the dark wood floor. I looked back at Bobby, and he was adjusting the driving gloves so they fit snug and tight across his knuckles. I could see the blue surgical gloves peeking out between the leather gloves and his long-sleeve shirt.

"He ain't got many more of those left in him, Bobby."

"Probably not."

"Then what?"

"Put him where nobody'll find him."

"And that's that? Won't be any questions?"

"There's always questions. I'll be fine."

You think you're walking away from this one, Bobby? Cops? Vargas? You think you drop Freddie in a hole and walk away?

Bobby looked at Freddie, tugging absently at his gloves, sliding the forefinger of his right hand into the groove between each of the fingers on his left hand so there was no slack at the tips. He looked up at me again. His eyes bored into mine then he shook his head and let a small puff of air out through his lips.

"Fuck, Ones, she was your girl. How did you let that go?"

"You too, Bobby?"

"What you mean, Ones?"

"You and Dasha?"

Even standing facing Freddie's slumped unconscious body, his shirt spattered in red and gore, Bobby smiled, the corners stropped to a straight razor's edge by grief so hard and tight that I wasn't sure the skin around his eyes could hold. He looked away. Shy.

"Yeah, Ones."

He looked up so I could see his eyes when he spoke.

"But after, Ones. Not during. Wouldn't do that. Can't say I wasn't feelin' it, but I didn't do nothing until you two were done. And she was shook up, Ones. Shook bad. Couldn't sleep, couldn't stop crying, but she said when she was with me, it was better. She was alright. She could breathe again. She was doing good."

I nodded.

"S'okay, Bobby. No hard."

He was looking at the floor again.

"I heard they found her. And it was on you."

He shook his head.

"Shoulda' known better. Wasn't thinkin' straight."

"No thing, Bobby. Nothing looked right."

Bobby looked at the body curled in the chair.

"Fucker knew how to tell it. Made sense at first. Wasn't 'til you came at me that I started really thinkin' about it. Didn't hold together."

He waved a hand at Freddie.

"Now we're here."

I didn't bother correcting him. Chucked my chin at Freddie.

"He mention Vargas?"

"Vargas?"

Bobby was surprised. Or good at faking it.

"What's Vargas got to do with this shit?"

"Wasn't just Freddie, Bobby. I think Vargas was in on it. I want them both."

"How does Vargas fit this, Ones?"

"Looks like he might have been in on it. Dasha took off their game, Bobby. Big money. Almost a million. Freddie set up the game, Vargas was a player."

Bobby ran a hand over his face and through his hair, standing it up in sweaty spikes.

"Fuck. I heard something went sideways at one of the games. Never figured it was Dasha."

"You knew about the game, Bobby?"

He didn't look at me, stared at Freddie.

"Sure. I worked it a couple of times. Easy gig. Two fifty a night, and everybody knew to leave the table alone—too many guys with weight in it."

Bobby ran his hands over his face again and reached behind without looking, found a chair and swung it around in front, straddling it, letting his head fall forward onto his folded arms.

"Fucking Dasha."

It felt like the room had let off a little air, like the walls had been taut against every joist, rage-strained, but now they had relaxed, settled a little bit.

"Yeah. Fucking Dasha."

There was a long silence. I could hear Tully breathing behind me and a thin rattle like pebbles on glass every time Freddie's chest dropped.

"So, who's your buddy?"

It came out muffled from behind his arms.

"Tools. He was in a couple of years back, but…meet Bobby V. Bobby, this is my buddy Tools. "

Tully held out his hand

"Bobby."

It wasn't bad, but I caught a tremor under the surface. Bobby held up both bloodied hands as if to have them inspected, then dropped them. Nodded at Tully and looked at me again.

"So. What now, Ones?"

I knew what I wanted to say.

"Really, Bobby? Beat the old fuck to medium ground in his own place, then ask me what's next? Really? Jail's next, you stupid fuck. Orange jumpsuits. Ankle cuffs. Talking to your mom through glass. That's what's fucking next."

I kept quiet for a few seconds, thinking. Not really—couldn't get any traction, thoughts rolling in my head like tumbling bingo balls.

"E?"

"Yeah, Tools?"

"This changes things. We don't have time now. Things have to happen fast."

"Things? "

"Yeah. I know. But we have to figure out what we're doing. And it has to happen in the next forty-eight hours."

"Forty-eight?"

"Give or take. We can keep the place shut down for a day or two, but if Vargas is in this, he'll be checking it out. Wondering what's going on. He finds this mess. He's going to be ready for anything."

I nodded.

"Okay. First things first. Let's get Freddie upstairs. There's a cot in the closet behind his desk."

"Really, Ones? He's in pretty bad shape."

"Get the cot set up. I think there's blankets there, too. Then we'll bring him up. Tools, can you give him a hand? Bobby, you got your blade?"

He leaned right, pulled it from where it was strapped along his calf, and handed it to me without looking over. He had taken off the driving gloves but was still wearing the surgical pair, and I could see where the right glove had split between the third and fourth knuckles.

He had used white zip ties, now smeared red with blood where the ties had cut into his wrists. Or maybe leaked down his back and onto the ties. I slipped the blade into one loop, a second, and a third—he was bound from wrist to elbow—and cut the ties. Freddie's arms flopped loose to his sides, and his body tilted forward as he came out of the chair. I reached up to steady him with both hands on his shoulders, one hand still holding the knife so that I nicked his chin as I steadied him, and the knife settled along his shoulder. Bobby looked at the knife resting near Freddie's throat, then at me.

"Give me a hand here, Bobby. Grab his shoulders."

He looked at me before standing up and coming around the chair to hold Freddie's shoulders. I moved around to the front of the chair and cut the ties that strapped him to the chair legs from ankle to knee. He shifted again when his legs came free, and Bobby had to strain to keep him in the chair. I grabbed at his right leg as it splayed to the side but missed, and Freddie's unconscious body slipped sideways off the chair and slumped to the floor with his left leg still draped across the chair.

"I'm not sure you gave that your best effort, Bobby."

"What you want? I throw myself at the floor, so he makes a soft landing?"

"I was thinking maybe hang on to him."

"Slippery fucker. "

"Tough to argue that."

"You boys doing okay here?"

Tully stood watching us from the bottom of the stairs—me on my knees in front of the chair, Bobby V standing his hands resting lightly on the back of the chair the blue surgical gloves now streaked with blood. He kept the tone light, but I could hear the strain running beneath the words.

"Not as good as it looks."

"Worse than it looks? Wow."

"Let's get him upstairs."

Tully walked over and bent to take Freddie under the arms. I stopped him.

"You take this end. No sense, both of us getting messed up, and I'm already bloodied."

We switched spots. I caught Freddie under the arms, and Tully caught him by the ankles and adjusted to hold him by the thighs. I backed towards the stairs, slipped on something wet on the wood floor and almost went down.

"You okay, E?"

I nodded.

"Slick spot."

We made it the rest of the way to the stairs.

"I think it'll be easier if I take it from here."

"You sure?"

"Yeah. Two of us and Freddie on these stairs sounds like an accident waiting. How you doing, Bobby? Played out, are ya'?"

He had settled on the ground beside the chair Freddie had been strapped into.

"Don't rag on me, Ones. I ain't carrying that motherfucker."

"Ain't that right, Bobby? You make the mess; we clean it up. Let's turn him over, Tools. I'll get him up over my shoulder. I should be able to get him up the stairs that way."

"What are you talking about, Flint? I was doing your fucking job.

This punk-ass kills your girl, jacks you up, and he's walking around like nothing happened. "

We both ignored him. Tully looked at me, waiting. I flushed.

"What are you waiting for, Tools? Turn him over."

"You sure, E? It makes more sense for me to carry him. Your bum knee..."

"Fuck, Tools, how many ways I got to say it? Turn him over."

It did make more sense—he was bigger, stronger, and didn't have a knee that occasionally gave like thin ice. But I could see that things were happening fast for him—he was having trouble keeping his hands still, rubbing first one arm then the other, running his hands back and forth through his hair, tugging at the skin on the inside of his wrists. I was pretty sure he wasn't up for having Freddie bleeding all over him.

We got him draped across my right shoulder, his face warm and wet against my lower back. He was heavier than I expected. The knee gave on the fifth step. It was like I has stepped through a trapdoor. I thought it was going to be OK because I pitched forward, but my good leg and Freddie's feet hit the step above me and bounced me back into Tully, who was following right behind. It caught him by surprise, and he rocked back, teetering on the edge of the step, trying to hold his balance against his own weight and mine and Freddie's I thought he had us, but the momentum was too much, and we edged past the tipping point and tumbled to the bottom of the stairs in a tangle of legs and arms.

"Shit. Fuck. Get him off me! Aww fuck!"

Something caught me in the lower back and knocked the wind out of me. I couldn't tell if it was fist or foot. I caught a glancing blow above my eye and another high on my hip, and it was over, me and Freddie tangled on the floor. Tully crabbing back, pushing frantically on his feet and hands, away from both of us. His face was white except around his eyes and where Freddie's blood had smeared his forehead and left cheek. There was a thick red wet line running from his shoulder almost to his wrist like textured paint.

"Fuck, E! Fuck! What happened?"

"It's okay, buddy. It's alright. My knee gave. You almost had us. It's okay."

I kept my voice low and even. I had never seen Tully quite like this. I had seen him frantic but not childlike and frightened like this.

"Jesus! Jesus! Jesus! What are we doing? What the fuck are we doing?"

"It's OK, Tools. It's going to be okay, pal. We're trying to sort things out for Dasha and Mya. Remember? Remember? We have to do this, OK? Reel it in, buddy."

I crawled over to where Tully was crouched, leaving Freddie sprawled at the bottom of the stairs, and put my arms around him, pulling his head into my shoulder and talking into his ear.

"Stay with me, Tools. I need you here, buddy. Breathe deep. C'mon, buddy, breathe. Bring it down now. Relax, it's going to be okay."

I could feel him beginning to calm, his breathing coming a little easier, and his body losing its rigid tension.

"Ones?"

L'il Mikey was at the top of the stairs. He spread his hands at the scene, Freddie splayed at the bottom of the stairs, Tully in my arms, Bobby V watching it all from the chair where Freddie had been bound.

"What the fuck?"

"Long story, Mikey. How did you get in?"

"Yeah, that's the craziest shit here, Ones. How I got in the building. Let's get that sorted out before somebody tells me why I'm standing in the middle a' some crazy-ass Reservoir Dogs shit."

"Right. Look, we'll tell you the story, Mikey, but we need to take care of Freddy first. Can you get him up onto the cot?"

He shook his head like he was trying to decide if he was even going to stick around but came down the stairs.

"He still breathing?"

Mikey bent low and nodded at me.

"Good. You OK to get him upstairs?"

He made a face and picked Freddie up with an arm under his shoulders and the other behind his knees like you would hold a child. He carried him easily up the stairs. I turned back to Tully. He was sitting with his arms, hugging his knees.

"You OK, Tools?"

He nodded. The color was coming back to his face, but he was still shaky.

"That was messed up, E."

"I know. Sorry. I thought the knee would be good for ten steps."

"I had looked away and when I looked back you were…he was coming at me. And for a second I thought I had caught you but I couldn't hold on and we were falling and his face was up against mine and the smell and the feel, slick and sour, and I could feel it on me…Jesus, it was gross."

I stood up and put out my hand, and he pulled himself to his feet.

"You good?"

He nodded.

We would see.

* * *

The four of us sat around the cot in Freddie's office. We had moved the desk out into the hallway to make room for the cot. Bobby V sprawled out in Freddie's leather swivel chair, his ass almost sliding off the front of the chair. L'il Mikey leaned against the wall, and Tully and I had found a couple of wooden chairs. We flipped them around, our chins resting on the hardbacks. I did most of the talking, but

Bobby would interrupt occasionally when I missed something. Mikey listened through the whole story, his face still and unmoving, not saying anything until we were done.

"I get why Bobby was here, but why you guys?"

He jerked his head at me and Tully.

"We were looking for Freddie."

"Bad timing. Why were you looking for him?"

"Wanted to ask Freddie about Vargas."

I looked at Bobby.

"He say anything about Vargas?"

"Didn't say much. And I wasn't really listening."

"Just going to beat him to death?"

"Hadn't thought that far ahead. Gonna' beat him for sure."

"I want Vargas."

Mikey spoke up.

"You don't know Vargas was in on this."

"He was in."

"You don't know."

I shook my head. He was right. I wasn't sure. Actually, that wasn't true. I was sure. I didn't trust myself.

"How do we smoke him out?"

"Smoke Vargas out? What are you talkin' about, Ones? You want him as far out of the picture as he can get. He come walking out of the smoke it'll be with two heads hanging from each hand."

Tully shook his head and scrubbed hard at a spot above his left eye.

"If your psycho friend hadn't beat the shit out of your boss, he could have told us."

Bobby looked at Tully but didn't say anything. Nobody spoke. I listened to the sound of Freddie's breathing, ragged and shallow. It didn't sound like it could go on for that long. I expect we were all listening. Maybe, not Bobby V. Tully's head came up.

"Fuck that."

Bobby V. Tully stared at him, then looked at me again.

"E? You got any way to get in touch with Vargas?"

"You got something?"

"Maybe."

I looked over at L'il Mikey.

"Can you get a message to Vargas?"

"Shit, Ones. How many times I gotta' say it? You don't want to mess with that guy."

"Too late for that, Mikey. First time Bobby smacked Freddie, we were hip-deep in Vargas. Just didn't know it."

"No fucking way. I didn't know Vargas was in this."

He stood up, moved into the hallway, and stood in the doorway to Freddie's office.

"This shit's too much for me, boys. I'm out."

"I know this is fucked, Mikey, and I wish things were different, but I'm not sure walking away is your best move."

"What the fuck you talkin' about, Ones?"

"You think Vargas' gonna' leave you outta' this? Once Vargas figures out what's gone down, he's gonna' assume you were in it. You're gonna' be part of the mess he has to clean up."

Mikey looked over at Bobby V for backup, and Bobby gave a half-headshake, half-shrug.

"Sorry, bra. He's right."

"Awww fuck. This guy's crazy. He never just shoots somebody. It's always like he owns a Home Hardware—blow torches and shit. Big ass electric sanders and nail guns and drills you gotta' crank by hand. It's fucked up, man."

Freddie made a small groaning noise, and we all looked over. He jerked twice under the thin blanket that Mikey had found with the cot, but his breathing settled. I swung back to Mikey.

"So?"

He looked away. I knew he was looking at the stairs that led up to the roof.

"This shit is messed up."

"Well?"

It took a few more seconds before it sunk in.

"There's a guy I can phone. Let him know I got something, and one of Vargas's guys will get back to me."

I looked over at Tully. He shrugged.

"Have to do."

"So? What're you thinking?"

"Get word to Vargas that we have info about the rip. That we know something about the second girl. If he's in on this, he's not going to give a shit…he'll know they already got the second girl. He'll blow us off. But if he doesn't know, he's going to want to talk. Hear what we've got."

I looked around the room, not at anybody, not trying to get a read—who gave a shit if they thought it was a good idea—trying to get my head around it.

"Pretty thin, Tools. The guy's a fucking lunatic—who knows how he'll react?"

Tully shrugged. It was all there in the simple movement—you got anything better? I didn't.

* * *

I stood at the top of the stairs, watching L'il Mikey talking on the phone across the room beyond the chair where Freddie had been bound. Where the blood had been smeared by people walking, it had dried a dull brown, but there were undisturbed spots where it had pooled and set, grown a skin like abandoned soup, but if I broke the thin film, it would spill again, settling into a smaller shallower pool that could be blurred across the floor with hand or heel to set and dry, without volume. Mikey spoke a few words, listened, then spoke again before nodding and hanging up. I couldn't hear anything from where I was standing. He stared at the phone and stuffed it in his pocket. He was almost at the foot of the stairs before he noticed me. His face didn't change, but he stopped.

"Ones."

"So?"

"He'll deliver the message."

"The what?"

Mikey shrugged.

"He'll get back to us."

I nodded.

"Or he won't."

"What does that mean, Mikey?"

"Shit, Ones, what do you think? These guys return all their calls? He'll do what the hell he wants. He wants to talk to you, he'll call. He doesn't, nada."

Chapter Seventeen

"He's going to die if he doesn't see a doctor, E."

The room was dark except for the glow coming from Freddie's computer monitor on the floor. There were no windows in the office, so we could have left the light on without giving away that we were there, but after Bobby had thought he heard something and flipped the light off, nobody had felt like turning it back on.

"I know."

"So"″

"If word gets out that Freddie's fucked up, Vargas is going to know something is up. We have to keep a lid on this. Until we sort out Vargas."

"Sort out Vargas. Shit."

He looked away, then back, and I could tell because the shadows shifted on his face like clouds scudding across a half-moon.

"And if he dies while we're waiting?"

"He won't die."

* * *

Freddie died before six in the morning. Tully worked on him for over an hour, but it wasn't something that could be fixed with CPR. I had seen it twice before now. Once, a bull rider took a hoof to the head—it took him three days to die when they couldn't relieve the pressure in his head. And a girl who I had hitchhiked with from Montana to Wyoming. The driver had been drunk. I knew it, could smell it when I leaned in the window, but it gets cold in Montana in November, and we had been standing on the side of the road for more than two hours. He tried to pass a guy on Eighty-Six outside Bozeman and didn't quite make it. We rolled three times. I was in the front seat, belted, and Sunny was sleeping across the backseat. I stayed with the car, and they found her about ninety feet away, still breathing. She kept breathing for almost a day, but her head had hit the ground too hard. They couldn't stop the swelling.

Freddie was the same. He had vomited twice during the night and had taken a seizure before vomiting the second time. Tully had slept for a few minutes during the night, and I had put a flashlight on Freddie's left eye, and it hadn't responded at all, the pupil filling the iris like a spreading stain so I could see almost nothing of the color of his eye. Not contracting at all when the light shone directly on it.

Who knows, maybe somebody could have done something for Freddie. But what he had done to Dasha? He'd given up access to mercy. At least, to mine.

* * *

Vargas called about thirty minutes later. I could hear Mikey's end of the conversation.

"Uh-huh. It's me."

"The girl. The second girl."

"I don't know."

"Einstein. Einstein Flint."

He looked over at me. Held out the phone. I took it from him.

"Yes?"

"Mr. Flint?"

I recognized the voice, the faint trace of an accent.

"Yes?"

"Why would I care about the second girl?"

I tried to read what was in his voice but couldn't get anything.

"Because you were at the game. You lost money."

"I see. What if I told you I don't care about the second girl?"

"Or the money?"

There was a long silence. Then,

"Meet me at the end of Pier Sixty-Two."

"When?"

"Noon."

"What do I get?"

"We won't find you and kill you."

I paused for a long time until he finally said,

"Well?"

"Fine."

"Alone."

"Fine."

I hung up and handed the phone to Mikey.

"He wants a meet."

"You going to do it?"

"Fuck no. But we have to do something."

Tully spoke first.

"He's in. If he was out, he would never have called back. Why call some crazy about shit you got nothing to do with? It doesn't make sense. Why get dragged in if you're not in already? He's in, and he needs to know what pieces are still on the board.

Tools was right.

"You sure?"

"Sure as I'm going to be. He killed Dasha, or called it. And he took

Mya out. He can't leave us wandering around."

"So, what do we do about the meet?"

I saw his head come up, hadn't realized in the dark that he wasn't looking at me, but now I could see the wet gleam of his eyes in the dimness.

"What?"

"Weren't you listening?"

"Listening to what?"

"Mikey and I went through this."

"Went through what?"

I took a deep breath, let the anger drain away as I exhaled, and walked him through the phone call. He didn't speak until we had finished.

"No way we're meeting with him."

"I agree. But it might be worth scouting the place, see who he brings with him. See if he comes loaded for bear looking to take us out right there. Maybe we can follow him, figure out where he's holed up."

"And do what? Take him out? What are you thinking, E? We're so far out of our league here, I'm not even sure we're playing the same sport. We need to find a deep hole, fall in, and pull the city down over us."

"He killed Dasha, Tully. You said so. And Mya. And we're going to look for cover?"

Tully took a minute, staring at me the whole time, before he nodded slowly.

"Can't hurt to know something. Where you want to watch from?"

"Could we see from the High Line?"

"Nah. Too far. And you shouldn't go—Vargas knows what you look like. He's never seen me before."

"I'm going."

"Right. It's no time to start doing the sensible thing."

"I'm going."

"Fine. But you'll need to stay out of sight. Pick a spot over on Pier

Sixty-One. I'll sit on the bench right at the entrance to Pier Sixty-Two. I'll be able to see them close-up."

"What are we looking for?"

I couldn't see him, but I could tell he was working at himself the way he does, tugging at the skin around his wrists, working his fingers back and forth through his hair, fastening and unfastening the button at his throat.

"If he comes…"

"Are you OK, Tools?"

"What? I'm good, E. I'm good."

"You sure?"

I could see the movement of his hands in the dark like silvered fish beneath the surface of the water, subtle shifts of shaded grey.

"It's OK, Tools. Just be straight with me."

"Little fucked up, E. Tide's coming in, but it's early. I'm good for a while yet."

"You take your meds?"

"Can't think on the meds. You know that, E."

"I get it, Tools, but it won't be any good if you go full-bore snakes and ladders, buddy. I need you with me here."

"I'm good, E."

"OK. So, what are we looking for?"

"If it's Vargas with a couple of guys for protection, there's a chance he's trying to figure things out—what you've got. That he doesn't know what's happening. If he comes in with a full team, looking to take us out…it means he's decided. When's the meet?"

"Noon."

"If you're really going, you should get there early. They'll be scouting the place. Don't want them spotting you wandering in. You should be on the pier by ten. I won't show up until sometime between eleven-thirty and twelve. They won't be looking for me, and I'll see them coming or going or both. I'll meet you at that little diner on Eighteenth Street at one. Don't hang around once we see them. Get a bead on how they're rolling and get lost. If they don't show by twelve-fifteen, leave. Wander around until it's time to meet up."

"What diner on Eighteenth?"

"You know the place—serves the great souvlaki?"

"It's on Tenth Avenue."

"Whatever. You know the place, I mean. Isn't it called something on eighteen?"

"Yeah. But it's on Tenth."

"This town is fucked up."

"Ones?"

"What's up, Bobby?"

"We gotta' get rid of Freddie."

"Sure, Bobby. Whatever you have to do."

Tully cleared his throat, and we both looked over.

"Bobby, let's clean up here first. When me and E head out for the meet you can take care of Freddie. Leave Mikey out of it. No sense having us coming and going more than we need to."

Chapter Eighteen

hey grabbed me up right at noon. Didn't see it coming. I was watching across the short stretch of water, not paying attention to who was around me, and didn't notice them until they were a step or two away. By the time it registered, one of them had the muzzle up tight against my back.

"Don't move, mi amigo."

My breath caught up short in my throat like a fish on a hook and it took a couple of seconds for it to come free and slide past my tongue and teeth. The next four or five breaths came in quick panting succession.

"Relax, buddy. Breathe deep. We've got your pal—the guy sitting at the gate. So don't think that he's gonna' be able to help you. Entiende?"

I nodded. My breathing was back under control, but I kept still.

"If you do anything stupid, we will dump you right here. You understand?"

I nodded again. I couldn't think. My thoughts scattered around my head like windblown scraps of paper. A guy moved in on each side, grabbing my upper arms, and the pressure of the muzzle left my side. I started to look to my right, but his voice stopped me.

"Eyes straight, amigo. Do what I tell you and it will be alright."

A woman off to my left, pushing a stroller looked over but quickly away—a survival reflex in New York. It must have looked a little off even if she couldn't see the gun. But it was over quickly, their car idling beyond the pier entrance. The guy with the gun dropped in beside the driver, and I was pushed into the car, and the two men who had been holding my arms bookended me in the backseat.

"What do you want with me?"

"Be quiet, Mr. Flint. Senor Vargas will explain."

I could see the left side of his ruined face. I hadn't recognized his voice because he hadn't spoken at Boom Boom's. It was high and breathy, a woman's voice except I had known it was a man, flat, without inflection or emphasis, the meaning carried in the words, nothing contained in the tone. I wondered if the voice was a by-product of what had been done to him or if he had always spoken like that.

"Vicente? When are w…"

The guy to my right.

"Shut up."

I kept my face straight ahead, looking through the windshield and cutting my eyes to his profile, the curdle of flesh covering the left side of his face. There was a spot the size of my thumb that ran along the ridge of his chin that looked like it had been left untouched, that was recognizable as human skin. A thin line of milky fluid slipped from the corner of his eye and caught in a raised scar above his lip. He dabbed at it with a handkerchief he had balled in his left hand. I looked to the front and he was watching me in the rearview mirror. I held his eyes, the right one clear and predatory the other, glazed, opaque, lifeless, then looked away.

"You mentioned my friend—I'm not sure what…"

"Please, Mr. Flint. No talking. Senor Vargas will explain everything."

"But I think there has been a mis…"

He held up his hand and the car pulled to the side of the road. We were driving north on the Henry Hudson, and there was almost no shoulder, so cars in the right lane had to move out to get around us. Several leaned on their horns but the man in the front seat ignored them. He turned and looked past me and nodded to the guy on my left, who opened his door, pulled me out, and pushed me up against the side of the car. The second man came around and the two men held me against the side of the car while the man with the mutilated face came around the car. He stepped in very close and I tried to pull away, but the men held me tight against the driver's door. I could see the suppurating places where the tissue hadn't completely healed, where it was moist and rose-red like a plague blemish, like the first sure sign he was going to die someday and he reached up into the narrow space between his face and mine and patted away the pus with his handkerchief. He had sweetened the cloth with something, and the mix of perfume and decay made me gag. He didn't move while I swallowed it back.

"I have asked you to be quiet twice, Mr. Flint."

And he punched me hard. He had to step back to make room, and I wasn't sure what was happening, but he buried his fist in my stomach. He may have sounded like Carol Channing, but I was pretty sure he didn't punch like her. I've felt worse pain, but I wasn't sure when. It had been many hours since I had eaten so all that came up was a thin streak of bile. The two guys straightened me up again.

"And you have ignored both requests."

That fucking voice. He hit me again. Same spot. It felt like something split. I would have dropped to both knees, but the men held me up. They had to bend and lean in to do it. I hung there feeling the acid rise in my throat again, letting it dribble across my lower lip and onto my shirt. He hit me twice in the face with shots I didn't see coming and I felt my nose give on the second. I must have been out for a bit because when I came around I was slumped over the trunk, my hips up on the back end of the car, my feet off the ground, blood, drool and puke mixed in a thin line gliding over the waxed metallic green surface. They pulled me to my feet. I found the scarred man and watched him. It would all come from him. He looked at me, holding until I looked away then he nodded at the men. They grabbed me so that they could lean me out into the road and pushed me forward so that I was facing the oncoming traffic. I watched the headlight of a blue Chevy van coming at me when they pulled me back again.

"Senor Vargas wants to talk with you. Otherwise, I would throw you into traffic."

They walked me around the car, my feet catching and dragging on the concrete, and slid me back into the car. I didn't speak again.

* * *

We drove for almost an hour, across the George Washington and into Jersey, turning off the highway once we hit the countryside, down a cracked asphalt road almost a mile to a chain-link fence blocking the road and caging a huge gravel area that could have held a couple of hundred cars and a warehouse with corrugated metal siding and roof. The fence was ten feet high and topped by another two feet of coiled barbed wire. The gate looked old, rusted but solid and when we were close it started to roll back. I couldn't see where the camera was, but somebody was watching. We pulled through the gate without having to slow, I twisted in my seat to watch the gate close and the pain doubled me over. He could hit. I listened as the gate closed behind us. We drove around to the back of the building, out of view of the road. There were two vehicles parked there, late-model American cars and a large roll-up door that could accommodate truck deliveries with a smaller wooden door beside it leading into the warehouse.

Vicente and his two guys left me inside with the driver while they were at the front of the car. Vicente moved to the smaller side door and it opened as he got close. I still couldn't see cameras—they had invested some money in surveillance. His two boys came and stood on opposite sides of the car facing away from the windows. I thought about tapping on the window to see if I could get them to bend and look in but settled for hugging my stomach with both arms trying to calm the pain in my gut. Vicente was gone for a few minutes when the big door began to roll back. I could hear the motor as the gears clanked into place and the door opened. Vargas was standing in the door. The sun was almost directly overhead so that Vargas's head and shoulders were still in the shadow cast by the door as it rolled back but I recognized him even before he took a step out into the full light. I had seen him a few times before at Boom Boom's, but, like those times, he looked good—his black hair combed back full and slick, an expensive mauve silk shirt hanging loose over tailored white slacks and what had to be hand-stitched snakeskin boots. He waved to the boys to take me from the car and took a look back into the darkness at something I couldn't see. I let them pull me from the car even though I was feeling better—not good but better. I had been stomped and bounced enough to know what was pain and what was injury. My gut was going to need a little repair—probably spleen, but the rest was pain. It would go away. But they didn't need to know that.

"Hello, Einstein. Do you mind me using your given name? We aren't old friends but nor are we meeting for the first time."

I nodded wearily—not needing to put much on.

"Excellent. This should not take long, Einstein. We simply need to know where the rest of the money is."

I shook my head, and a thin stream of bile flipped from my nose onto the shirt of the guy holding my right arm. I looked up at him and shrugged.

"Sorry, pal, didn't see that coming."

He grimaced but didn't loosen his grip on my arm. Vargas snapped his fingers.

"Over here, Einstein. The money."

I shook my head again.

"Don't know anything about no money. Just know the other girl—the one who helped out with Dasha."

"Please, Einstein. Don't make this more unpleasant than it has to be—we know who the second girl was. What we don't know is where you put the money."

Fuck.

"No sense holding back, E. I already told them the money's in my room."

Tully. I couldn't see him back in the shadows, but it was him.

"How're you doing, buddy? They must have worked you pretty good that you gave it up already."

"Shut up! Both of you."

"Yeah, these boys don't mess around, E. My head feels like ten pounds of pork in a five-pound bag."

Vargas nodded at somebody behind him, and I heard a wet smack followed by a low groan.

All I wanted to do was cover the thirty feet between us and take him off at the neck, but there was no way I was getting free, and it was better if they thought I was feeling worse than I was. I let my knees go and slumped against the car, and the two guys had to bear my weight to stand me up. Vargas waved them forward. I left my legs slack, and they had to drag me across the tarmac. I let my chin loll down onto my chest so that my head swayed from side to side with every step. I hadn't noticed the sun, but now I could feel it warming my neck and head. They stopped, and I slivered my eyes open enough to see the tips of Vargas's boots. He slapped my face twice, each cheek, not hard, lightly like he was scolding an inattentive child.

"Look at me, Einstein."

I played it wide and deep, dragging my head up as if it was a great weight so I could look at him, my eyes slits but open. He nodded, his face pleasant but not smiling.

"We want the money. Then this can be finished. You and your friend can go home, and we can forget this unpleasantness."

I nodded, tried to look over his shoulder into the dimness. Vargas waved his hand at me.

"He is fine, sore but unharmed."

"Let me see him."

Vargas spoke over his shoulder.

"Tell your friend you are fine."

Tully's voice was firm and steady, but I could hear the control it took.

"It's alright, E. A couple of these guys can throw them pretty good but no permanent damage. I couldn't hold out—they know the money is in the air vent in my room at the hospital."

I heard the sharp smack of a closed fist on loosened flesh and the thin hiss of pain through clenched teeth. I let my chin fall back to my chest and had to catch myself not to jerk my head up at the sound.

"Your friend is a talker, Einstein. He's still figuring out how much talking is OK."

"What do you want from us?"

"We need you to pick up the money."

"Us?"

"Not 'us'. You. It's not likely they will let us poke around in your friend's room. But you, they would. We'll hang on to your friend. Vicente? You take Einstein to the hospital. He will pick up the money and return with you in the car."

Vicente nodded, and Vargas turned back to me.

" If you do not come back with the money, we will kill your friend, then find you and kill you slowly."

Tully had bought us some time but not much. And giving them the money wasn't the answer—the cash was the only thing between us and bleeding out in a deserted warehouse. But I had no idea what would happen when I came down without the money. Actually, I had a pretty good idea…he had just told me.

"How you doing, Tully?"

Vargas backhanded me before Tully even had a chance to answer, catching me across the ear and cheek. I could feel where his ring had split the skin below my eye, and there was a loud buzzing in my head so that, for a second, I could see Vargas' lips move, but couldn't hear what he was saying. It came back like a transistor radio finding the signal.

"…ame, Einstein. Bring us the money and live."

"Let me see my friend."

"He's right, E. Bring them the money and live."

It was all there in the tone—the same sardonic drawl he always used when he repeated something ridiculous.

"There ain't no cavalry riding in to help us on this one."

Letting me know that we needed to get help. But from where? Had to be Evans. Bobby and L'il Mikey might help but even they would have to think twice about going up against Vargas. And how?

Vargas looked at Vicente and jerked his chin towards the car I had come in.

"Get the money."

Vicente nodded and eyeballed the two guys holding me. They spun me around and dragged me back to the passenger side back door.

"Just a moment!"

They turned me around to look at Vargas. Two of his guys had walked Tully out into the light and left him standing, swaying, looking at me through the eye that was still open enough that he could see. There was a red blotch where his lips and teeth had been; a pale pink snot bubble rose from the center of his face as he exhaled, then disappeared as he sucked air back into his lungs, coughing hard and almost falling as blood spray got sucked down his windpipe. Vargas nodded at the bigger of the two men, and he threw a hard overhand right, effortlessly, like sliding his arm into a suit jacket, and Tully went down like a wet towel sliding off a clothesline.

"Every hour until you get back, Einstein. Be as quick as you can."

* * *

We were double-parked across the street from the hospital. We had been sitting there for several minutes while Vicente looked at the entrance, and then at me in the rear-view mirror. Finally, he opened his door, stepped out, followed by the guy to my right. He leaned in and dragged me onto the sidewalk, yanking me hard to my feet when I stumbled. Vicente hissed something at him in Spanish that I didn't understand, but I guessed was a reminder that we were in public and that he should avoid attracting a lot of attention.

"Okay, Mr. Flint, you and I will go in and get the money."

I grinned. Didn't feel like it, but we had one chance, and only if I went in there alone.

"Sure. Me and you. We'll walk in and up to the room of the runaway psych patient, slip in, grab the money, and slip back out undetected. That shouldn't be a problem. Nobody will notice us—a torn-down gringo and…"

I waved my hand at his face.

"…and this. It's a long shot that I get in on my own, but dragging you along will be an absolute no-go. Guaranteed."

His good eye narrowed. He spoke in Spanish to the guy on my left—I could see where this was going and shook my head.

"Won't work. On my own, I might be able to pull this off. No guarantees, but there's a chance. I've been in and out of this hospital a dozen times; people are used to my face. One of your guys? Look at them; they set off alarm bells standing beside the car…how do you think it will go when they try and tiptoe through a locked-down psych ward?"

He shook his head, but I could tell he was almost there.

"What are you worried about? That I duck out the back door? You've got my buddy—I'm not running. And how far could I go? "

He stood angled slightly so he could stare at me, and I held his eye. It was hard not to let my glance shift to the glistening droplets that he dabbed away with the stained cloth as they oozed up through the broken, damaged surface of his face. Finally, he nodded.

"He will kill him. You understand?"

I had no doubt. I nodded without speaking.

"I'll need to clean up."

"Yes, you will."

There was a MacDonald's on the same block, and Vicente and both his boys came in with me while I washed up. There wouldn't have been any need if it had been left to Vicente—he had left no marks that you could see, but Vargas's backhand had left blood soaked into my shirt collar and a thin black-red line running from the thick, red scab under my eye down my cheek and neck to the place where it disappeared beneath my shirt.

I washed my face and chest, working gingerly around the puffed gash, and tried to soak the stain out of my shirt collar, but Vicente impatiently pointed at the smaller of his guys to give me his shirt. The guy's eyes widened but Vicente stared at him until he took off his shirt. It was black and silk and too big for me, but it worked OK with the jeans. My shirt on Vargas's guy looked like a game-show prank, the sleeves ending a couple of inches below the elbows, and the shirt pulled taut across his chest, gaps large enough that tanned hairless skin could be seen.

Vicente looked me over and nodded.

"You have fifteen minutes to find the money and come out with it. If I don't see you in fifteen minutes, I phone and deliver the message that your friend be killed. Then we come after you."

"What if I get stopped?"

"That would be unfortunate. For your friend. And for you."

I looked at him but couldn't think of anything else to say, so I turned and walked across the street and up the walkway into the hospital. The reception desk was at the south end of the hallway and couldn't be seen from the street. There was a slim East Indian woman behind the desk, but by the time I made it to the desk, I was behind a middle-aged woman holding a small child who was probably her granddaughter. The little girl stared up at me. I crossed my eyes, but she looked down and away at the floor. It took four minutes for the woman to get her questions answered. The little girl didn't look at me again even as they walked away.

"Can I help you, sir?"

I had been watching the little girl. Shit, I had to get my head back in the game.

"Can I use your phone to make…"

"I'm sorry, sir, this phone isn't for public use."

"Do you have a public phone?"

"We did…

She waved over my shoulder.

"…over near the restrooms, but everybody has a cell phone now, so they came and took it away."

"This is an emergency, ma'am.

She looked doubtful.

"Really. Nine-one-one. Can I please use your phone?"

She pulled it up and placed it on the desk, still looking doubtful. I did hit nine-one-one. I couldn't think of a better way to get through to Evans.

"Hello. What is your emergency?"

"I need to talk to Detective Evans. He's at the Seventh Precinct…"

"I'm sorry, sir, this is an emergency line—we don't direct you to other police departments."

"This is an emergency. I need to speak to Detective Evans right now, and I don't know his number..."

"I'm sorry, sir. What is your emergency? We can send police officers to the scene..."

"I don't need police officers—I need one police officer...Detective Evans. Could you just..."

"I'm sorry, sir. I'm going to have to ask you to clear the line if you don't have an emergency. We..."

I hung up. I could see the face of the woman's watch from where I stood—I had six more minutes. The woman behind the desk reached for the phone, but I held up one finger and curled my left arm around it.

"One more call. I swear."

The phone number I could remember was Freddie's private line. L'il Mikey had a cell, but I couldn't remember the number. By the third ring, they would all be looking at the phone. The Boom Boom's bar phone had probably been ringing off and on most of the morning, but Freddie didn't give his office number out to that many people. By the tenth ring, I could imagine them staring at the phone, waiting for it to stop. No fucking way. On the thirty-second ring, I heard it pick up. Nobody spoke.

"L'il Mikey?"

There was a long pause.

"It's Bobby."

"Bobby. It's you. That's great. Look, man. Listen up, I don't have long. We got scooped up by Vargas and his guys. Me and Tully. Both of us. "

He tried to interrupt with questions, but I cut him off.

"I need you to get ahold of a cop named Evans. He's a detective in the Seventh Precinct. He was the guy your boy went to with the story that I had put the finger on Dasha. Tell him Vargas is the guy that offed Mya and probably Dasha, too. He has…"

"Where are you, Ones?"

"Doesn't matter, Bobby. Vargas grabbed us up. He was waiting for us. We're going to be taking him to that place on Broome off Bowery—you know the hotel, I mean? We're in room 338. Let Evans know that's where we're headed, and Vargas's guys will be with us."

"I don't get this, Ones. What the fu…"

"I don't have time to talk anymore, Bobby. Get ahold of Evans. And it's got to happen fast. We'll be there in an hour or two. Tell him not to take us to the hotel, follow us back to warehouse if he wants to take down Vargas."

"Ones? Wh.."

"Gotta' go, Bobby. Remember Evans and the place on Broome. We'll be there in an hour, two at the most."

Bobby was still talking when I hung up. I looked at the receptionist's watch—one minute. Now, things got tricky. I had to convince Vicente and Vargas that we weren't shining them on and that the money was at the hotel. I wasn't sure how to do that.

"Thanks."

I spun away from the desk and headed back towards the door and out into the street. Vicente and his boys were standing at the curb watching the door, and I knew he wasn't going to be happy to see me empty-handed. But you couldn't tell. The guy was good. As I walked across the street, he eyed me up and down without changing expression. Although it was hard to say how many expressions he might have.

"Where is the money?"

"It wasn't there."

"That's not good."

"There was a key."

"What kind of key?"

I pulled our hotel key out of my pocket.

"A hotel key. I'm guessing Tully moved the money and hid the key up in the vent in his room."

He took it from my hand.

"Why didn't he tell us?"

I shook my head.

"I don't know. Maybe he was hoping there was a still a way we could hang on to the money."

"That was very foolish."

"I know it was, Vicente. But it's a minor detour. We go to the hotel and pick up the money. It's all good."

"What hotel?"

I shook my head.

"This was Tully's thing. He must have made the switch when we weren't together."

He turned the key over in his hand—it was an actual key, not a card—but there were no identifying marks.

"I will talk with Raul."

I let my head drop. He nodded at his boys to put me in the car and moved around to the passenger's side.

* * *

There was no dramatic backlit stance in the open rollback this time. They hustled me out of the back seat and into the warehouse through the narrow door beside the truck entrance. Vicente had talked with Vargas on the way back in the car, but I couldn't hear what they had said. My goal was to keep both Tully and me alive until we got back to the warehouse with the money. If the cavalry didn't show up by then, it wouldn't matter anyway.

Tully was tied to the chair again, and it looked like he had taken a couple more shots. I couldn't tell if he was conscious, but I went at him as soon as I got through the door. They weren't expecting it, and I might have made it to the chair if I hadn't slipped on something wet on the floor. Good thing. The two guys grabbed me and pulled me back while I screamed at him.

"You fucked-up, tweakin' motherfucker. What the fuck are you doing? The money wasn't there! They're gonna' kill us! Don't you get that? If they don't get the money, they're going to kill us."

His head rolled up from his chest. I could see a narrow glint where one eye was open, but I couldn't even tell where the other eye was. He tried to smile, I think, but his lips were so torn it was tough to be sure.

"Right. Forgot. Moved the money. Shit."

I could barely understand him. I brought it down a notch. Still shouting but tamping back the hysteria. It was tougher than I expected.

"Stop fuckin' around, Tools—tell them where the money is, and let's get this done. Tell them what hotel the key's for."

Tully's head had been rolling back and forth on his chest, but when I mentioned the key, it stilled for a moment, a held breath, and started again, a thin line of pink drool running from the corner of the red mash that was his mouth to a spot on the shoulder of his shirt, stretching and retracting with each sway of his head.

Vicente and Vargas had been standing behind me, but now Vargas stepped forward into my line of sight, holding the key in his right hand.

"What is this, Mr. Tully?"

Tully spoke to me.

"You piece-a-shit loser. I get you out of here, alone in the hospital, and you crawl up, find the key, and bring it back to these fucks? Couldn't make a run? "

"Mr. Tully, your friend understands the gravity of your situation. You do not. Now is not the time to squabble among yourselves. Now is not the time for daring escapes. Now is the time to tell me what hotel the money is at and what room in the hotel."

"That's our money!"

Vargas shook his head as if disappointed in a stubborn child.

"It was never your money. It was always my money. Whether you held it. Or the girls held it. Or Mr. Flint...Einstein. Held it. It was always my money."

"Fuck you."

"Tell him where the money is, Tools."

"Fuck you, too."

"Tools. Don't do this. Tell him."

He shook his head. I knew what he was thinking. It couldn't be easy, had to be hard. Or they'd start to wonder. I wasn't sure Tully could do much harder. Vargas nodded, and one of his boys, a guy who had been leaning back against the wall in the shadows. He wore dark pants and a black sweater, but I could still see the subtle changes in shade where Tully's blood had splashed his clothes.

"Wait. Give me a word?"

I didn't wait for Vargas to answer.

"Give it up, Tools. They can have the money. Let's get out of this."

He didn't look up at me. It was as if he hadn't heard me.

"If you don't tell them, I'm going to start making some wild guesses."

He looked up at me. I watched it drain out of him. He had been holding hard, but I had given him a way out, and he wanted to take it. Bad. He nodded.

"Okay. Fuck. SoHotel. Room 417.

He looked at me when he said it, but it was Vargas that spoke.

"That's good, Mr. Tully. This had better not be a second goose chase."

"Wild goose."

"What?"

"Wild goose chase. Not goose chase."

"Let it go, Tools."

"Nah, E. They can get this shit right, at least. Fuckin' goose chase? Shit."

Vargas looked at him for a long time, then gestured to Vicente without looking away.

"Take Mr. Flint. Get the money. If there is no money, take one of his eyes."

He looked at me.

"The right one. Then bring him back here, and we will get to work."

I had to make a conscious effort not to rub my eye. Vargas turned back to Tully.

"And you will watch, Mr. Tully. Every second. If we have to staple your eyelids open."

"You better not be fucking with them here, Tools."

He didn't look away from Vargas, his eye glittering in the folds of bruised and swollen skin.

"It's there."

"Better be."

"Or what, E?"

He was selling it pretty hard.

* * *

It was a quiet ride to the hotel, the traffic starting to pick up, so it was slow going. I tried to talk to Vicente a couple of times, but he ignored me. As we approached the hotel, I looked for signs that Bobby had gotten through but didn't see anything. I wasn't sure what I expected—if they weren't slick enough to fool me, they weren't going to fool Vicente. Vicente had the driver pull up to the building and got out.

"Circle the block until we come back out."

The guy to my left spoke up,

"You want us with you, jefe?"

"No. You stay with the car. Get him out."

The guy who had spoken popped the door, pulled me out, and slid back into the car. Vicente took me by the arm for the first few steps.

"Don't fuck this up."

I couldn't think of anything to say to that. Good intentions hadn't helped me so far. The woman at the reception desk looked up when we came in, but when she saw we were heading straight for the elevators, she looked back down at the work in front of her. The lobby was empty except for an older couple standing beside three pieces of luggage inside the door. Waiting for a cab. Didn't look like cops. We were the only ones waiting for the elevator and rode it in silence to the fourth floor. We had shoved the backpacks into the closet inside the door, and I had a moment where I imagined that the cleaning staff had taken us off, but when I slid the doors back, they were both there, one on top of the other. Vicente gestured for me to open them up, and I did, letting him see the pile of bills.

"Empty them."

"What?"

"I want to see all the cash."

I shrugged and dumped both of the backpacks upside down, letting the cash tumble to the floor. It made a jumbled mound almost to my knee. Vicente nodded.

"Pack it up again."

"Shit, Vicente."

"Do it."

I packed the money up again and zipped up the packs.

"OK. Put them on. One on the back, one on the front."

"You don't think that's going to look strange?"

'Put them on."

I shrugged into the first pack—felt like thirty or forty pounds and slipped the straps of the second pack over my shoulders so that it rested against my chest. I could feel the weight on my bad knee, but it was bearable. We made it down the elevator and through the lobby without attracting much overt attention. It was New York—a guy wearing two backpacks was the seventeenth most unusual thing you would see in any one-block stroll.

We stood at the curb, waiting for the car to circle the block. I looked up and down the block—the usual traffic in the streets and on the sidewalks, but nothing that looked like help. Nothing. It was something I had always loved about New York—that it was so alive, there was so much going on, but it happened all around you. Nobody paid you any attention. Now, I was praying that somebody was watching, that I was imagining the same old feeling that I was an invisible spectator.

What was I looking for? Somebody in a trench coat tapping the side of his nose? Nothing. That was what I should want to see, but it was starting to feel like there was nothing. The Town Car slid up next to us, and the shorter guy got out, tossed the backpacks into the trunk, and pushed in beside me when I got back in the car. The car slid out into traffic, and we started the last leg. I wanted desperately to look behind for headlights but knew it was a bad idea and didn't matter—there would be headlights, no way of knowing whether they were help.

* * *

The traffic was as bad going back, but the drive felt short. It was the same as the first time, the gate topped by razor wire rolling back as we approached, the car not having to stop or even slow. We pulled in tight to the wall so that the packs could come out of the trunk and right in the side door of the warehouse. I stood to the side as the driver and the shorter guy grabbed the backpacks from the trunk, and Vicente held me back, so I entered first, and he was the last of the five of us.

The warehouse was lit by three rows of lights hanging down from the high ceiling. The floor was dirt, hard-packed, and the building was more than a football field deep. Tully was tied to a chair about forty feet in from the loading dock entrance, a guy on each side. Vargas stood leaning against the loading dock door, watching us. Tully looked even worse than I had expected, his eyes swollen full shut, his nose smeared across one misshapen cheek, his lips as wet and ragged as chewed tobacco. They had been working on him while we were gone.

He swung his head up and towards us at the sound of the door, but it was a little off the line of sight, not landing quite right.

"That you, E?"

It was thick, a little hard to understand, but he got it out.

"It's me, partner."

"Any luck?"

"Got the money."

"Don't imagine that will get us out of here."

"Wouldn't think so."

Vicente had moved up close to Vargas, talking low, his mouth almost touching his boss's ear. I couldn't hear what they said, and neither man looked over…until the very end , when Vicente placed his hand on Vargas' arm before stepping away, and Vargas's eyes shifted to where I stood, measuring me. Not what I was capable of, how large of a space they would need for my body.

I listened, straining for any sound, but all I could hear was the wet rasp and flutter of Tool's breathing and a thin scrape as one of Vargas's men shifted his feet on the rough concrete floor. There was nothing out there but the dark and a thousand places to bury us. The fear rose like flood water in my chest, and the exhalation caught up hard against something in my throat. My mouth opened and closed as I tried to push air, but it stayed wedged in my esophagus as thick and solid as a piece of unchewed meat; feeling like if I could force the air bolus past the block and over my lips, it would tumble, clot wet, to the floor. The air grayed. His voice floated across the space between us. I wasn't even sure he was still awake, still conscious.

"BTW, big man."

It had been our motto, something only a couple of teenage kids could tell each other and mean. But we had carried it ever since. We had talked about it in the dark for weeks, lying in our beds, trying to figure out how to deal with what was coming for us. Emotional alchemy. Bring the Wrath. Chew and swallow every scrap of fear and spit it back as rage. Gather the thin blades of terror that whittled you down to something you wished you couldn't recognize and wind them, twist them into a barbed hammer. And we had never spoken about it again. Other than BTW. It had got me on the bull a dozen times. The worst that could happen is that you died angry.

Something gave in my chest, and the air came in a rush. My vision cleared, and I expected Vargas and Vicente to be watching, wondering what was happening, but they hadn't noticed me. They had both moved closer to Tools. I shook, vibrating like a tapped tuning fork, but they were looking away. I breathed deep, trying to rein myself in, not give in completely to reckless anger.

"What did you say?"

Tully's head tilted as if he was looking at them, but his eyes were so swollen that I doubted he could see. He shook his head and let it fall back to his chest but didn't speak. Vargas nodded at Vicente, and he took a step closer.

"What did you say to your friend, Mr. Tully?"

"What now, Vargas? We got you your money."

He didn't look over, but it stopped him.

"Yeah, sure. We'll drop you off at home now."

I took a few seconds to answer.

"How did it go, Raul?"

He looked at me now.

"You thought you had her beat, ready to pop, one last twist, and she'd spill? Didn't go that way, huh?"

I laughed. It was easier than I thought it would be.

"That girl was tough, son. You could have peeled her one layer at a fucking time, Raul, and she wouldn't have given you a fucking thing."

I rolled the R long and trilled, then let the u drag.

"Didn't feel like you thought it would, did it, Raul? She almost buried you. Three more seconds, and you're in the ground, and she's spending your money. That's how close it was."

He took three long steps across the floor and drove his fist into the middle of my face. Not a bad shot, enough to break my nose, but he hadn't planted solid, and it was mostly arm. I took two steps back before catching myself. I could feel the swelling right away and spit to clear the blood in my mouth. Tears welled, and I couldn't stop them.

"She'll come for you, Raul. If she can, she'll come for you. I know you know that. You were in the room. You looked in her eyes. What was she afraid of, Raul? I wasn't even there, and I know what she was afraid of—she was afraid she wouldn't live long enough to eat your heart…wouldn't have a chance to stick her arm down your throat and pluck that little grey mouse from your chest and swallow it whole."

He hit me again, and this time I went down. I could have stayed up. He was strong and fast, but his technique wasn't great. But I wanted him thinking I was almost done. Don't get me wrong—it hurt. And I was getting pretty tired of being punched in the face. But mostly, I was glad Vicente wasn't giving the beating—I had a hunch he could have put me out with one careful shot. I spoke over Vargas's shoulder as I got to one knee, playing it weak, almost tipping over but catching myself.

"Hey, Tools? Can you imagine this punk and Dasha in a fair fight? Shit, she would have made him her girlfriend."

I slurred the words and nodded my head as if I was trying to clear it, but I was thinking as coherently as I had in hours. I had seen the bulge under his shirt when Vargas had been leaning against the wall. If I could get him close, confident, I might be able to grab the gun. It wouldn't matter. There were four more of them, and they all had guns. And Vicente was a pro, there wouldn't be any panic there—he would take me out, then count the bodies. But it was better than closing my eyes and taking one to the side of the head without complaint, might even be able to get a bullet or two into Vargas.

"What you think, Tools? Think Raul would have danced for Dasha?"

I had staggered back three or four steps before I went down, and Vargas started to follow me. Vicente spoke,

"Raul."

"Callate, Vicente."

But it slowed him. One more step, and I would come off the floor fast, drive my shoulder into his gut and grab for the gun. I tensed my leg…

The lights went out. Vargas took another step, and the lights went out. I'm not sure what was supposed to happen next, but whatever it was, it wasn't likely as good as the lights going out.

I came out of my crouch but not in the original direction I had planned, veering slightly right towards Tully.

It's deep water black. I can't see anything, but I hear them milling around, Vargas's voice and a voice I don't recognize, one of his goons cursing in Spanish in the dark, and the sound of the light switch being flicked on and off several times and another curse.

I found him in the dark, bumping hard into the chair, hitting it hard enough so that even with Tully's weight, I almost knocked it over. He gasped low and sharp. I crouched behind the chair, found his hands and the zip ties binding them. He must have been working on them for a while, but the ties were wedged tight across his knuckles.

"Pull."

He said it, quiet and fierce. I pulled. I felt a knuckle pop, and the tie slipped down his hands, slick with sweat and blood.

"The door!"

That was Vicente. If they could get the door open, they could get enough light, even at night, to corral us.

"Que?"

One of the goons. I moved around to the front of the chair and felt around at the bottom of the chair legs. His ankles were bound snugly to the chair legs. I pulled at the ties, but there was almost no give. I leaned into his ear.

"Can you stand up?"

There was a pause and I felt the slight change in airflow as he nodded. I held the chair tight to the floor as he tried to stand. It took three tries, and while Tully struggled up, I could hear them talking in loud whispers, trying to get to the door and get it open. We didn't have long. On the third try, I pushed hard between his shoulder blades, and he tipped, almost falling forward before the ties caught him. I jerked hard upwards on the chair, hearing him gasp every time until the legs pulled free and he crumpled to the ground. I felt around until I found his face, my hand slick and warm from the snot, blood, and sweat, and leaned in close again.

"Back corner, Tools."

I didn't get a response as far as I could tell, but he tried to help, pushing off with his legs as I pulled him up from under his shoulders. Once he was standing, I got his arm around my shoulders, swung my right arm around his waist, and we staggered deeper into the warehouse. There were two ways out of the warehouse that I had seen: the loading dock door and the small door beside it. They weren't options for us. Tully could barely lift his feet, and the scrape and skid as we dragged across the gritted concrete floor sounded loud and damning, but they were talking now, giving up on the whispering, although all I heard was a jumble of voices and cursing.

We were two-thirds of the way across the floor when they got the side door open. I looked back, and the moon bled enough light that I could see dark shapes silhouetted in the door frame. But the light was soaked by the dim and dark within six or eight strides of the entrance. Soon enough, they would get the loading dock door fully open, and we needed to be buried in the back corner before that happened. I kept Tully moving even as I heard them working at the door, the hollow sound of the loading door button clicking on and off, and Vargas speaking angrily in Spanish.

We took nine or ten more steps before coming up hard against the back wall. I hadn't seen any change in the shading as we approached, and I hit it hard, banging my broken nose off the corrugated metal. My head spun, and I thought I might slip under, but stood for a moment until the spinning stopped.

"Can you keep moving, Tools?"

He patted me on the shoulder but didn't speak. I shifted to his other side and worked along the back wall until we reached the corner. Tully was gasping when we got there, and it sounded loud in the air around me. I lowered him to the floor, settling him on the hard-packed dirt where the concrete had run out as we approached the back wall. I sat down next to him. Vargas, Vicente, and the other three were still gathered at the front of the building, but they sounded like they had given up on the loading dock door. They was a long, quiet moment,

"Mr. Flint?"

It was Vargas.

I didn't have a plan. Nothing. I had run for the dark. That was it. Stay out of sight. In a building the size of a football field. We had delayed the inevitable. Unless somebody was coming. That's what I was counting on—that the power going out was the first domino to fall.

"Flint?"

He shouted it out, and it echoed off the corrugated metal walls.

"What can this do for you? You think we won't find you in here? Or maybe we'll take the money, get in our cars, and drive away?"

His voice hung in the air and faded.

That won't happen, Flint. "

He was talking too much. And a shadow was missing.

"You're right, Flint. You're not walking away from this one. Not you or your friend. But it can end easy or hard. If we have to come find you it's going to go slow and hard. If you walk in right now, it'll be quick and easy. One behind the ear."

I was listening, straining. Vargas's guy might come across the floor, but it seemed more likely that he would follow the wall—he would feel safer and he would expect us to be along the wall. But I didn't know from which direction. I greyed, the blood pounding in my head and my own breathing loud and rasping in my ears. Dasha. If she could see this she would be laughing—might feel a little bad but wouldn't show it. I could hear her. "Dumbass...I fucked up and got shot—you should have kept walking, Ones." I shook my head, and snot or blood, probably both, flipped across my cheek, and my head tilted. Even dead, she managed to mess me up.

I sucked deep, forcing air past the tightness in my throat, the pounding in my head receding. The guy wouldn't be long finding us, and...the scrape of material on concrete rasped like a struck match in the dark and quiet, and I stepped into him. It's all that saved me because I think he must have heard me at about the same time and was bringing his gun up. He pulled the trigger, but I was inside his arm, and he shot past me—I hoped Tools had stayed on the ground. The light of the muzzle flash flared, and he was there, then gone.

I kept coming, spilling both of us into the dirt. He went down hard and off balance, and I followed him down. His breath was hot and loud in my ear, and I brought my head back then forward, hoping to break his nose, but he turned, and I caught him on the ear. It had to hurt, but he grunted and bucked against me. He was bigger and stronger, and he hadn't been taking beatings like they were vitamins for the last week—if he had come straight at me, it likely would have been over quickly.

But he must have dropped the gun when I hit him, and now he reached out with one arm trying to find it, using the other hand to push at my face, trying to bend my head away from him, trying to create enough space so that when he found the gun, he could push the barrel up against my body and pull the trigger. I clamped both my legs around one of his and put both hands into his face, clawing for his eyes but missing, my thumb driving up one nostril. I pulled as hard as I could and felt the flap of skin holding his right nostril to his face, give and tear. He screamed and bucked harder.

I hung on, but he had given up on the gun and was punching with both hands. I took a hard shot high on the temple and felt myself flip, almost going under but hanging on. It didn't take much. I lost my grip, and he was on top of me, driving shots down towards my face and neck. It was still black dark so most of the shots were missing or sliding off my raised arms, but I had no doubt—it was a matter of time if I couldn't get free. He was going to pound until a shot landed flush, and it would just be how long they wanted it to take.

I twisted left and then came back hard to the right but he anticipated it and shifted his weight and caught me with a punch high on the forehead that caused light to splash behind my eyes. The next one scraped across my cheek, not hitting flush but hard enough that it split the skin where Bobby V had already cut me. I felt him straighten and tense above me, and I brought my head forward and to the left, and I heard his fist drive by my ear and into the ground. He swore in Spanish. I ducked in the other direction and caught another glancing shot that caused me to tilt-a-whirl.

The gunshots caught me by surprise, and I thought at first the guy had found the dropped weapon and shot me. I had never been shot before, so I didn't know if maybe the shock of being shot left you unsure if you had been hit. I had seen that in the movies, guys coming out of a gunfight and not realizing they had been shot until they touched the wound and saw the blood on their hands. Sounded like bullshit to me, but you never know. The lights came on. The guy on top of me had frozen at the shots, and when the lights came on, he shielded his eyes and looked towards the front of the hanger.

I could hear shouting voices. What I was pretty sure was Bobby V shouting at somebody in Spanish, then more shots and the ratcheting as the loading dock door slid up.

I looked to my right and saw the guy moving along the back wall. He had found his gun, and it hung at his side as he worked along the back wall, watching the scene at the front of the building. He had forgotten us. I turned my head to look, too. I could see two bodies on the ground, one moving, trying to stand, and the other still as stone. There were three men standing in the door firing out into the dark, not trying to take cover from return fire. Two, standing straight and still firing like they were at the range and the third crouched and shooting. I looked back to the guy along the wall, and he had made the corner and was now sliding along the long side wall. I turned on my side and spun loose for a second before coming to. I looked to the wall, and he had moved several steps along.

He hadn't seen me yet, and I got myself up on all fours, feeling the room tilt and spin, letting it settle before I pushed to my feet. I noticed that the shooting had stopped. The guy along the wall spotted me, looked towards Bobby and the two shooters in the doorway, and held his finger to his lips. I grinned back at him. It was funny how when things got bad, I couldn't help smiling. Some kind of weird reflex. It wasn't like I thought anything was funny.

"Bobby."

It came out thin and parched but loud enough that he turned in the loading dock door and looked over his shoulder. He spun around when he spotted me. I nodded at the guy along the wall, and Bobby shifted his gaze. The guy had started to bring his gun up. I couldn't tell if he was going to point towards me or the door. But when he saw Bobby look his way, he let the gun fall back to his side, then let it slip onto the concrete, the clatter echoing loud in the sudden silence of the hanger. The other two turned at the sound, and the guy on the left snapped off a quick shot that clipped concrete free a foot to the left of the guy along the wall, and he shrunk back, holding a hand up to ward off the next shot.

"Fuck, don't shoot."

Bobby spoke first.

'Little quick on the trigger there, partner."

"Shit, where did he come from?"

"Problem with you white boys is you watched too many cowboy movies."

I recognized the voices, Dwight and Evans, and settled back to the ground, one hand straight-arming the floor to keep me sitting. I looked to the other corner, and Tully was slumped against the wall, legs splayed straight, and his head lolled to one side. I couldn't tell if he was awake or even alive, but his tongue came out and licked at his torn lips, and I saw the thin shine of his left eye through the swollen tissue.

"You alright, Tools?"

He said something I couldn't make out.

"Didn't catch that, buddy."

It was hard to understand, but I got it this time.

"Still here."

I nodded.

"You hang tight. I've got to go talk to the boys."

But I couldn't stand up. I waited until they came and got us.

187

Chapter Nineteen

L'il Mikey had to carry Tully out. I was able to lean on Bobby V and make it to the door. Vargas and Vicente had made a run for the car after their two boys went down. Vargas was behind the wheel, blood soaking the front of his shirt from the gaping bullet wound in his neck. He looked posed, like those shots of bank robbers in true crime magazines, but it was how it happened. He had made it to the car and behind the wheel but didn't get a chance to close the door. I looked in through the open door and saw the keys on the floor beside his foot. Hadn't had time to shift them to his right hand to get them in the ignition.

Vicente hadn't made it to the passenger side door, hanging back, trying to cover his boss. His body was slumped against the back bumper, three or four red stains on the front of his jacket and a seeping hole over his right eye. It wouldn't look as tidy at the back.

I must have passed out.

Chapter Twenty

They kept me overnight. Tools was five days and some reconstructive surgery on his right eye. I'll admit it: I wondered what Dwight and Evans would do about the money. Almost a half a million dollars—it's a lot of money. But they played it pretty straight. Not completely straight—they kept L'il Mikey and Bobby V off the books. Said they didn't want to jam them up, but I was pretty sure they would have had their own problems if the brass found they had teamed up with a couple of civvies.

They got to us in the hospital—tell the story straight—the way it happened. Except it was Dwight and Evans that broke things up. Bobby V and L'il Mikey were out of it except for calling it in. Wouldn't be hard to sell that. The bad guy still walking was the guy that had messed me up, and nobody would believe his story even if he decided to tell it. Word was that he ended up pleading out to a short stretch—so maybe they cinched that by making a deal. I didn't give a shit what happened to that guy, Bobby V had hit me harder, and I wasn't looking for him to do long time.

* * *

The four of us sat along the rail. Only getting up to walk around the bar and pull one from the fridge when we finished the first. I looked around the room.

"What's going to happen to the place?"

"Hard to say. Can't do much until they track down Freddie."

"What's the word?"

"They figure he beat it when he heard about Vargas and Vicente."

"How long's that gonna' hold?"

Bobby V shrugged, looked across me, and Tools to L'il Mikey. He shrugged, too.

"Who knows? Might hold."

"Any chance he's going to pop up somewhere?"

Bobby V shook his head.

"No chance. That one's gone."

"Won't they wonder when he doesn't touch his money? His bank accounts?"

"Ol' Freddy wasn't much for bank accounts."

Mikey didn't look up from his beer when he said it. I waited.

"Kept most of his cash in the safe behind his desk."

"Okay. So, won't they be wondering why he didn't touch that money?"

L'il Mikey looked a little sheepish and still wouldn't look up from his beer. But I was starting to get the drift.

"Safe was empty."

"Empty, huh? How did the cops get in?"

"They bring in a guy. Took him about four minutes once he found the right drill bit."

"And when they opened the safe, it was empty?"

"Yeah. Some paperwork but no cash. A little red book where he kept track of receipts. They figure he's carrying a little over a million."

"Right. But you gotta' tell me."

There was a long pause before Mikey looked up at me and down the bar to Bobby V. Bobby gave a short nod.

"Freddie wasn't so good with remembering numbers. Kept his

passwords and shit taped under his desk."

"How did you find out?"

"A waitress."

"How did she…Ahh, fuck, I don't want to know."

We sat for a few seconds without talking.

"So, what you gonna' do, Mikey."

"Doesn't make sense to shut it down. Far as everybody knows right now, I'm running it until things cool down."

I nodded.

"Sounds about right."

L'il Mikey took a long draw and put the bottle back on the bar.

"You lookin' for work, Ones?"

I let one hand move to my face and rub across the new ridges and furrows.

"Feel like I could use a break. At least, from the beatdowns."

Mikey nodded across the bar.

"I'm gonna' have to spend more time upstairs—you want the bar? Pretty sure you'll screw it up, but at least I'll know I'm not getting skimmed. Money's a little better and you let Bobby and the boys take care of the knuckleheads."

I looked at him, then down at the bar.

"Thanks Mikey. I'd like that. When you want me to start? I may have to heal up."

"No problem. I'm gonna' shut down for a week or so, get my act together. Say, a week?"

"That works, Mikey."

He looked over my head.

"What about you, Troy? You looking for work? I just lost a doorman."

Tully looked at me, then across at Mikey.

"You sure I'm the guy for the job? "

He shrugged.

"What? You lookin' to audition? Don't really care if you're kicking their shit or they're kicking yours… so long as you're not getting any on the paying customers. That mess all over your face gonna' scare most folks for a while."

"Sounds good, Mikey. I'll take it."

We sat without talking for a while, the only sound the quiet scrape of bottles off and on the bar. Bobby stood up.

"I got a place to be. You boys okay?"

I nodded.

"We're good, Bobby."

Mikey stood up.

"I'm done, too."

He slid the keys along the bar.

" You OK to lock up, Ones?"

"Sure. You fine with that?"

He looked around the room this time.

"You gonna' screw it up?"

I shook my head.

"Nah. I think I'll leave it alone."

The guy made me smile.

"Drop the keys at Shady's."

"No problem, Mikey."

They left, and we sat and listened to the quiet padding of their feet down the stairs and the dull click as the outside door closed behind them. I held up an empty, and Tools nodded—I went behind the bar and grabbed a couple more. We were almost done before I spoke.

"How you feeling?"

"Not bad considering."

"So, pretty bad?"

"Yeah, pretty bad. But it's getting better."

We sat for a little in the dim of the bar.

"How did you keep it tight back there, Tools? It looked like you were already starting to go even before the shit went down."

He shrugged and tapped his head.

"It's a fuckin' chemistry experiment up there. And I was hurting bad, E, no doubt about that. I was messed up. But everything stayed connected, none of the wires crossed. There were a couple of times when I wondered if it might be better to be dead. But I was thinking clear. When you get hit that hard, and you're that scared, maybe things straighten out for a bit."

"How about now?"

He shrugged again.

"Remember what you said about what to do when you get an easy ride?"

I nodded.

"Sure. Ride easy."

He gave a soft, slow grin.

"I'm riding easy, partner. Can't last, but I'll take it while it's here.

Acknowledgements

Thanks to Shawn and all the folks at Level Best for your hard work on *Boom Boom's Last Call.*

About the Author

Jeff Houlahan was born in Calgary, Alberta and grew up on a series of military bases in Canada and Germany before settling in Ottawa, Canada. He has been a waiter, a security guard (there is nothing less hip than being a nineteen-year-old security guard in full uniform at a midnight showing of *The Rocky Horror Picture Show*), a bartender, made pool liners (a much tougher job than it sounds), delivered mail on Parliament Hill and played guitar in a punk band called The Rainkings.

Along the way, Jeff had a short post-doctoral stint with James Brown, one of the great ecologists of the last 50 years, and the third most famous person with that name. But, for folks with a literary bent, Jim's greatest claim to fame is that he was Barbara Kingsolver's M. Sc. supervisor at The University of Arizona. Barbara received her degree sometime between 1983 and 1985 and published *The Bean Trees* in 1988, so there is a chance that book was in the works while she was studying with Jim.

Today, Jeff lives with his wife Kim in Saint John, New Brunswick and is an ecologist and conservation biologist at the University of New Brunswick. All along he's been writing—short stories, songs, and, over the last dozen years, novels. In 2022, Jeff's first novel, *Long Train Home*, was published by Level Best Books.

SOCIAL MEDIA HANDLES:
 Email: jeffhoulwrites@gmail.com
 Facebook: jeffhoulahanauthor
 Instagran: jeffhoulahan
 X: @jeffhoul

AUTHOR WEBSITE:
 jeffhoulahan.com

Also by Jeff Houlahan

Long Train Home (Level Best Books)